Heroes & Villains: A Col
By Mark R
Published by Ma
Copyright 2019 N

Table of Contents
Prologue
Sapphire
The Mighty Mindweaver
Stalking the Prey
The Unstable
Energy Man
The Fighters
The Masters
Terminator X

One Man Battalions
Strike!
Terak

Phase: The Threat of Monsters
Strato
Nemesis
Energy
BOLTS!
Battle Crew
The Warriors
The Scarabs
Starforce & the Mystery of the Sphynx

The Blasters
Part 1
Part 2
Part 3
The Razors vs. The Thrashers
The New Blasters vs the Crashers
The Newest Blasters

Unbelievable Titan

Versus
Sergeant Wrath vs Red Devil
Freedom Fighter vs Killer Alien
Fighting Kid & Mr. Rock N Roll vs the Agents
Firestones vs Icecaps
Mr. Destructo vs Super Ant
The V-Men Battle Royale

The Beasts
Air Ace
Krickey Man

Space Stories
Kulos!
Space Ninja
Spaced-Out with Thrasher
Phaser

Executioner
Warriors of Justice vs. Death Squad
Planet of Death
Bi-Leap
The Murder of Big Dan

Myths
The Myth of Volcanoes
The Myth of the Bermuda Triangle
The 13th Labor of Hercules
Baldness and Aging-A Native American Myth

IF
A Wild, Crazy, Scary Adventure
The Ghost
Mighty Heroes in Training
The Drug War
The Battle Over Ice Station Cobra
The Hidden War

About the Author
Connect with the Author

For my family

Prologue
We all are busy. So hopefully the reader has time to read short, entertaining stories. I have adapted these short stories from comics that I had drawn as a child up through high school. Hopefully you enjoy these stories that stemmed from my young imagination. I must confess that I watched a lot of action movies as a kid. For the most part, I have chosen to maintain the integrity of my stories by not changing much of them.

Sapphire

A ship is soaring through space, near earth. The ship was in a space battle and is on its last leg. Because of the valuable cargo, the ship is going to self-destruct. With seconds remaining, the pilot ejects in a small ship from the larger ship.

While a few hundred feet in the air above eastern Tennessee, a large bird slams into the windshield, distorting the pilot's view.

The ship dips closer to earth. An old couple sees the ship slowly gliding near their home.

"Hey Paw! Get the shotgun!" the old lady squawks.

The old man fires a buckshot and it hits the tail of the ship. The pilot increases speed and altitude.

Shortly after, Arnold Air Force Base in Tullahoma, Tennessee sees the ship on their systems.

"It's a UFO!" a young soldier exclaims while seeing it on his screens.

"Shoot it down!" demands his commanding officer gruffly.

A blast from a high-powered machine gun hits one of the wings. The ship spirals out of control and crash lands near Knoxville.

A man in his early thirties sees the pilot get out of the ship, staggering to his feet. The man runs over and lightly puts his hand on the pilot's shoulder from behind.

"Hey buddy…" the man says. "What the…" he continues as he sees the alien face.

The man moans then shouts in surprise as power enters his body, merging the soul of the pilot with the man's body. A large Sapphire is now embedded in his chest, glowing with energy.

"Ahh dude…" he says.

Then the power takes over.

"I must stop criminals here on earth and help people as I can," the man says, as if in a trance.

The man has now become Sapphire. Sapphire feels something in his chest. He learns that he has energy powers.

"Oh no." he says as he flies into action with a blast of light. He arrives in Philadelphia within minutes.

Sapphire sees and feels the presence of an evil being nearby. The evil being can create large, man-eating plants and can control them. They are rooted in the pavement. A man screams in fear as the evil plant grabs him with its strong, thorny vines.

Sapphire quickly enters the sewers just below. Using blasts of energy, he fries the roots of the creatures, thus frying the beings above ground. He then smashes through the street above him and lands nearby, crouching.

A gang of thugs approach.

The leader says, "Hey team...looks like we have a super nerd!"

Then they crowd around him, clutching knives and baseball bats.

Sapphire slowly rises to his feet. POW! Sapphire blasts energy around him, engulfing the small crowd. He then walks away, their lifeless bodies strewn about, smoke billowing from their corpses. Suddenly, a ship fires at him from above. He dodges. The ship uses a homing device and sucks him in.

A moment later, Sapphire finds himself strapped to a table. An armored guard watches over him and clasps a small laser cannon in his hands.

"He could be very useful!" exclaims the ship's leader from nearby.

Sapphire smashes through the metal cables that hold him. He punches the guard, causing the guard's helmet to fly off.

The leader uses his power over electricity to shock Sapphire. But Sapphire then blasts into the electricity with his own power, forcing it back.

Sapphire uses his power to armor up. He smashes the leader with his fist, then absorbs the leader into his Sapphire, shrinking and trapping him.

The leader smashes out of the stone in Sapphire's chest, then grows back to normal size. Sapphire causes the stone to reform on his chest.

"Guards!" the leader yells as he charges up his power, his hands glowing. He fires at Sapphire, who dodges at the last second. The blasts hit two guards, one firing wide and missing Sapphire with a blast from his gun.

Sapphire slams the leader in the chest with his fist, causing the leader to groan in pain.

A mutant blasts Sapphire from behind. Then Sapphire bows and firmly crosses his arms as he glows with energy, thus giving him more power.

A new group of men crowd around Sapphire. One leaps through the air toward him with a knife. Sapphire quickly grabs the flying man out of the air and throws him into the small crowd. He kicks both feet into the chest of another. He slams two together by their heads.

A muscular, sharp-toothed giant, named Cruch, aims a large rifle and fires. The blast hits Sapphire in the chest. Sapphire groans in pain. The alien presence leaves his body.

"Nice one! You'll get a raise!" says the leader.

Shortly after and elsewhere, the alien presence enters the body of a skateboarder. Sapphire then gains armor with his power. He is coasting down the street, his hands glowing with power.

As he is passing a bank, a criminal is running out with money as he is shooting people with his gun. Sapphire blasts him with his power.

"I hurt all over!" the criminal screams, then explodes into several pieces.

Sapphire then tosses the bag of money back to a bank employee.

He then finds a hideout and works on his armored suit.

Hours later, word spreads of Sapphire.

Deathchaser, the leader of one of the criminal groups in the area talks to his men. He has an eyepatch, a mullet, and a large rifle.

"I want his head! Ready boys?" he asks.

"Sure," growls a large monster-like creature that is brandishing a scimitar.

"Sure, boss!" says a large man with a rifle strapped to his back and carries a sword and shield.

"I am always ready!" a red ninja whispers.

Shortly after, the criminals track Sapphire down. The large monster-like creature lurks in the shadows as he sees Sapphire skateboarding by. He leaps toward him and swings his sword, slicing off Sapphire's backpack.

Sapphire then hurls two Shuriken which rip into the creature's chest, killing it. Sapphire then starts to skateboard away. But his time boarding is short-lived as the large man with the sword swings and slices his board in half as he is boarding by. Sapphire blasts the giant in the chest. The giant groans in pain and falls flat on his face as he dies.

A shuriken knocks Sapphire's helmet off. He looks up to see the red ninja crouching on the roof of a small building nearby. Sapphire then flies up and grabs the ninja by his outfit and throws him to the ground, adding extra strength with his powers. The ninja slams into the pavement, blood splattering upon impact.

Sapphire then sees a sniper on a nearby building, with his rifle aimed at him, ready to fire. For a split second, Sapphire is in the crosshairs. Sapphire quickly fires a laser blast, hitting Deathchaser. The blast blows apart the head of his enemy.

The End

The Mighty Mindweaver!

One day, a man named Jeremiah Stone was riding past a nuclear power plant on his motorcycle. He saw that the power plant had lights flashing and alarms blaring. A man had come out into the street and was screaming for help.

Jeremiah hastily threw caution to the wind and scrambled into the building to see what he could do to help. A man was inside near the radioactive core and was having a hard time moving. Jeremiah helped the man, but the radiation had hit him. Suddenly, the radiation stopped. At that moment, Jeremiah knew that he had gained superpowers.

He had gained telekinetic powers and decided to use those powers to fight crime. He now calls himself the Mighty Mindweaver.

That was months ago. He has now met a new threat. He is riding past a cemetery and comes across a being that is called Kestrel. This demonic villain is summoning the dead from their graves. Mindweaver jumps into action.

"Hey! You! You've gone too far!" says Mindweaver.

"What did I do?" says Kestrel.

"You made people come back to life. You don't have the right to do that!" says Mindweaver as he punches Kestrel in the face. He then throws a dagger that hits Kestrel in the shoulder.

"Kill him. Then you're free!" says Kestrel to his minions telepathically.

A zombie silently creeps up behind Mindweaver and grabs him by the neck from behind. The zombie then punches Mindweaver, sending him flying. Mindweaver realizes that Kestrel was controlling the zombies, so he pulls out his two six shooters and shoots Kestrel four times in the chest, killing him. The zombies retreat to their graves.

Part 2-Skullstalker

Mindweaver buys more guns and ammo, an arsenal to be exact. He wants to be ready next time.

"Need a bag?" the gun store owner jokes.

Meanwhile, an evil man has escaped from a high security prison. He had pilfered a heavy machine gun.

"Come on! Come on, coppers! Can't you do better?" he screams at a police chopper as he shoots it down.

Shortly after, he guns down three people in the streets, as if he is a wild game hunter.

"That's 30 points," he crows.

Days later, Mindweaver sees on TV that this fugitive, calling himself Skullstalker, is calling him out.

"You're next, Mindweaver!" he says.

"You wish," whispers Mindweaver as he crushes a nearby empty soda can with his mind.

Hours later, dressed in a fedora and a trench coat, Skullstalker is walking down the street. He bumps into a homeless man, on purpose, more than likely.

"Excuse me," mumbles the hobo.

"Wipe your chin…it's got blood on it!" says Skullstalker as he grabs the man and fires several rounds into the unfortunate man.

Skullstalker calmly tosses the corpse into a garbage can, then straightens his tie as he walks away.

Meanwhile, not too far away, Mindweaver is trying to track down Skullstalker, but is just finishing off a carnivorous alien, ripping its arm off with his telekinesis after he had fired several rounds into its chest from his 9mm.

A crowd has gathered and is amazed at what had just happened.

Bullets slam into the pavement near Mindweaver as he dodges, just in time. He sees Skullstalker and glares at him.

"Up against the wall!" screams Skullstalker.

"Okay…" says Mindweaver.

Skullstalker fires his machine gun and blasts the weapons out of Mindweaver's hands.

"Don't move!" growls Skullstalker.

Mindweaver cooperates, but then Skullstalker fires multiple rounds into Mindweaver's chest. Mindweaver collapses. If it wasn't for his powers and his light armor, he would have died.

When he comes to, he finds that some of the crowd had done what they could to help him. Mindweaver happened to have a small first aid kit, so he quickly patches himself up. But he felt that his powers were drained.

"Where did he go?" Mindweaver says to the crowd.

"Into the sewers," one man says.

In the sewers, Mindweaver uses his flashlight to look around. He didn't have to look far to find a trail of carnage and destruction. He finds three dead homeless men, then a trail of bloody footprints. He treads on, sheer determination driving him forward.

Then, after about 15 frantic minutes of searching and hunting through the water in the tunnels, he sees Skullstalker. Mindweaver wants to keep quiet, so he throws a knife. But Skullstalker saw it coming and blasts it out of the air with his gun.

Mindweaver whips out his machine gun and fires. Skullstalker dodges the barrage of bullets. Skullstalker picks up the knife and throws it, missing Mindweaver. Skullstalker runs away.

Minutes later, Mindweaver sees Skullstalker climbing a ladder to the surface. Mindweaver fires his machinegun and the bullets graze Skullstalker's thigh and calf on one leg. Skullstalker limps down the street. But a drunk driver hits him with his car. Skullstalker passes out.

Later, Skullstalker is tied up and at Mindweaver's headquarters. Mindweaver roughs him up. He then takes him back to the police, who then put him into a maximum-security prison. This time for life, without parole and in solitary confinement.

The End

Stalking the Prey

Tygro has a mystical sword and he is a master swordsman. He also has the strength and senses of a tiger.

One day, while walking down the street incognito in the city, unbeknownst to him, he is in the sights of a hitman's sniper rifle. The hitman has been tracking him. The hitman's name is Skullstalker. He had recently escaped from a maximum-security prison. He had joined some other villains. He has transformed. He became more of a monster as he now has sharp teeth. He was also given a powerful, mystical stone which has given him powers. It is embedded in his forehead.

Skullstalker fires his automatic sniper rifle but misses his target. The bullet hits an innocent bystander through the head, killing him.

Tygro quickly rips out of his clothes, whips out his sword, and is ready for action.

Skullstalker leaps out of the nearby window, shattered glass filling the air. He nimbly lands a few dozen feet from Tygro.

"You're dead, tiger man!" he yells with determination as he fires his rifle but misses again.

He then uses the stone and causes a throbbing pain in Tygro's head. He then leaps toward Tygro. Tygro swiftly dodges, then raises his sword to attack.

Skullstalker aims his rifle and is readying a shot.

Suddenly, a woman in a hoodie emerges from the shadows and hurls a small dagger at the hitman. With perfect aim, the knife enters the gun barrel, jamming it. In a fluid motion, the woman then hurls a set of bolas and grabs Tygro by the arm.

"Let's get out of here!" the woman says hurriedly to Tygro.

The bolas cause Skullstalker to fall. As he is falling, the woman is running by and roundhouse kicks him across the face.

Skullstalker screams maniacally with fury as he struggles to get loose.

Tygro and the woman run at top speed down a nearby alley.

"Do you have a death wish?" Tygro says to the woman.

"You looked like you needed saving from that monster of a man. And I thought you were cute," she says between gasps as they run.

"My name is Tygro. What's yours?" Tygro says.

"Camille," she says.

After running several blocks, they make it to a wooded park. They find a place to hide and to catch their breath.

"Who are you and why does he want to kill you?" Camille says as she pulls back her hoodie, revealing a homely face.

She then pulls off her disguise, revealing very attractive features.

"To answer the second part, I am not sure." Tygro begins with a smile.

Then, with a flood of memories flashing through his head, Tygro tells her his origin.

"I grew up in South America. As a teenager, I contracted a flesh-eating virus. I was near death. My parents were able to get me experimental treatment from a small yet affluent pharmaceutical company. It involved a mixture of steroids and the DNA of tigers. It mutated me. Initially, I felt like a monster. I now have heightened senses and increased strength. But now, I guess you could say that I am more of a wanderer."

"What's with the sword?" Camille says.

"I enter tournaments in sword fighting to earn money to survive on. Just over a year ago, I won the largest tournament in the world and this was my prize," Tygro says with a gleam in his eyes.

"Your turn. What's with the disguise? What's your story?" Tygro asks.

"Off the record, I'm on the run. I have been off the grid for about a year now. I was in with the wrong crowd and into drugs. I came home one day to find my place trashed and all my roommates dead. I feared for my life, so that's when I started running," Camille says.

"We should go," says Tygro as he takes off toward another part of the city.

"What's the plan?" Camille says as she takes off after him.

"Let's go to my place. It's on the roof of an office building."

In the distance, Skullstalker emerges from the shadows.

"The pharma company wants to collect on your treatment…" he whispers under his breath as he slowly stalks toward his prey.

Minutes later, Tygro and Camille are at Tygro's place. They are standing on the roof, peering over the city while having a drink.

"This is an amazing view," Camille says as she stands near the edge of the building and looks out over the city.

Just as she turns toward Tygro, a gun fires, bullets whizzing at her. She turns and falls off the building.

"Nooo!" Tygro roars as he pulls out his sword.

Skullstalker, who is only a few feet from Tygro, is about to fire again.

Lightning fast, he runs at Skullstalker.

In a fluid motion, Tygro slices the hitman's gun in half, then stabs him through the heart.

"WHY?" Tygro growls.

"The treatments for you were unpaid…" Skullstalker says as he collapses and dies in a pool of his own blood.

Tygro quickly runs to the side of the building. Camille is laying on a fire escape, gasping in pain.

They get her to a hospital.

Tygro and Camille have a relationship. Camille gets her affairs in order. But at least, in the back of Tygro's mind, he wonders if the pharmaceutical company is still after him…

The End

The UNSTABLE

The Unstable stands at the top of a building like a gargoyle statue. He is called the Unstable because his powers are, well, unstable. Suddenly, bullets smash the ground around him, but he dodges. Quickly, he draws his sword. He sees Birdman in a helicopter looming before him. Birdman is his nemesis and is a psychopath that can control birds. He wears an old, tattered bird mascot outfit. His presence is haunting.

Birds fly out of the helicopter and attack the Unstable. Our protagonist punches the birds. He then jumps and kicks Birdman. But then he falls. Quickly, he fires claws from his gloves that are attached to very fine, but very strong wire. The claws catch on a nearby building, so he swings and smashes through a window.

As he is leaving the building, an armored robot of Birdman approaches. The Unstable kicks him in the face. The robot fires a machinegun blast from its wrist, hitting the Unstable in the chest. The hero has just enough strength to decapitate the robot with his sword. The wound in his chest heals.

A muscular henchman jumps through a nearby window, brandishing a small machine gun.

He fires at the Unstable. BRAP! The Unstable dodges, then punches the henchman squarely in the jaw, knocking him out.

Another enemy approaches. It is Carcass, a co-conspirator of Birdman. Wearing all black, he has an old, skeletal face. One of his hands glows with power. Carcass blasts the Unstable, freezing him in place.

Shortly after, the Unstable is taken to Birdman's headquarters. Birdman cackles with glee as he grabs the Unstable. The Unstable punches Birdman in the face, knocking his mask off.

Birdman fires from his gun, but the Unstable quickly blocks it with his sword.

"Cooperate...I need you to stand down from trying to stop us from achieving our plans," says Birdman.

"...or else!" says Carcass.

From his gloves, the Unstable fires pepper spray into Carcass's eyes.

"My eyes!" he screams, then punches the Unstable in the chest. Birdman knocks out Unstable with a pistol whip to the back of his head.

Minutes later, the two villains chain Unstable to the wall. One of their cronies proceeds to torture him with high voltage from a prod. After one shock, the Unstable grabs the crony with his feet, forcing the crony to shock himself, then the weapon hits the chain, causing it to come free from the wall.

"STOP!" says Carcass as he blasts the Unstable in the chest.

"Ahhhhhh!" the Unstable screams, then quivers and moans.

His clothes rip apart and he grows claws and hair as he transforms into a werewolf.

"GRRRR! Why did you torture me? WHY?" he growls as he lifts Carcass up by the throat.

"I…a…uh…I had to…yeah!" squeaks Carcass as he grins sheepishly.

The Unstable slams Carcass down and rips him apart.

BAM! A bullet slams into the Unstable's back. He turns to see Birdman sneering in triumph.

"You're an easy target!" Birdman cackles with glee.

The Unstable transforms back into a human. He unsheathes his sword threateningly. Quickly, he charges and slashes into Birdman's shoulder.

Birdman fires his gun and grazes the Unstable's shoulder. The Unstable punches Birdman in the head as he slices into Birdman's side, killing him.

The Unstable leaves town and is never seen again.

The END

Energy Man

- "Good people do not need laws to tell them to act responsibly, while bad people will find a way around the laws." - Plato

Dallin Grant, also known as Energy Man, is walking down the street. Other than his glowing necklace, he looks like an ordinary person.

As he is walking past a dark alley, four gang members emerge.

"Hey man, give us that necklace!" one says as he pulls out his knife. "NOW!"

Energy Man talks as he attacks… "Over my…" Energy Man punches the attacker in the face, "…dead…"as he kicks him in the crotch, "…body!" he says as he uppercuts him.

"Oh yeah, tough guy?" says another as he pulls a gun on him.

"Yeah!" says Energy Man as he kicks the second one in the belly.

He grabs this one by the jacket and says, "Tell them to quit or you'll get a bloody nose!"

"Get him!" says the gang member defiantly.

"Shut up!" says Energy Man as he slams him with both fists in the face.

ZAP! A surge of power envelops Energy Man, transforming him and giving him strength and energy power.

Another gang member says, "It's just a costume!"

"No, it's not," howls Energy Man.

The third gang member fires his gun at him. Energy Man destroys the bullets in midair. With a scream of anger, the third one pulls out a sickle. Energy Man blasts him with his power.

The fourth one, who looks very strange as he has a Mohawk and a monocle, fires his heavy machine gun.

It grazes Energy Man in the shoulder. Energy Man punches him, then blasts him. He decides to leave, so he flies off.

As Energy Man is flying, he reminisces about how he had acquired his powers a few weeks ago.

He was with a friend and they were racing each other with their motorcycles. As they came upon a power station, they had both lost control at the same time. They both slammed into a power plant during a meltdown. They both received powers.

Energy Man decided to use his powers for good. His friend, Kamron Ryker, on the other hand, decided to use his powers for evil. Kamron had mutated into a monster, growing horns, claws, and sharp teeth.

With an E emblazoned on his chest, Kamron has now become Evilkill.

Coming back to the present, Energy Man hears something from below a split second before Evilkill slams into him.

Levitating in front of him, Evilkill extends his claws and screeches, "I'll kill you, man!"

Energy Man punches him. They hear a loud rumble. Down below, they see two small armies assembled. One of cloaked swordsmen and the other is an army of winged demons.

It is clear which side Energy Man and Evilkill will join. A vicious battle ensues. After several minutes of fighting, Energy Man faces off again against Evilkill. Energy Man uppercuts Evilkill.

Seeing that Evilkill is charging up to send out a blast of energy, he puts up a force field around him. Evilkill unleashes a massive blast of energy, killing most of the remaining armies.

Energy Man is generating power in his hands while Evilkill extends his claws. Suddenly, Energy man is tackled from behind. An enemy fighter holds up a sickle and is about to strike.

Evilkill howls with delight.

Energy Man fires a blast that vaporizes his tackler.

Evilkill attacks by slashing across Energy Man's face.

"To the death!" screeches Evilkill as he holds up his claws threateningly.

"To the death," says Energy Man holding up a fist.

Evilkill claws at him but misses. Energy Man grabs him by the wrists then uppercuts Evilkill, sending him flying backward.

Energy Man fires a blast, hitting Evilkill in the chest, knocking him down. Smoke billows from the villain's chest.

"You were my friend! Why did you have to go off the deep end?" Energy Man says pleadingly as he walks away.

Evilkill sends a blast which blows off Energy Man's cape as he dodged at the last second.

Energy Man fires another, more powerful blast, which vaporizes Evilkill. Energy Man flies off.

The End

The Fighters

The Fighters were a group of thirteen adventurers that fought evil. But after a group of nine of their enemies had ambushed them at their headquarters, only three remained:

-Armor-With his powerful armor, he can fly, fire blasts from his hands, and has superhuman strength.

-The Sword Brothers-Kristian and Ryker are masters of the sword, unmatched with their skills. Their swords are magical, being able to cut through nearly anything.

A massive robot is sent to finish them off. Armor blasts it in the face as the Sword Brothers slash apart an arm and hand of the behemoth with their mystical swords.

The bot swats Armor away. It then fires a blast at the Sword Brothers.

Armor sees that nothing is left of them as he is flying after being slammed by the enemy. He hits the ground VERY hard and is knocked out. Minutes later, he regains consciousness.

"NO! My friends!" he screams in anguish as he flies after the robot, following a trail of destruction.

Mustering his power, he flies and rips one of the robot's arms off by flying and smashing through it.

Meanwhile, inside the robot, while Armor was knocked out, a demented scientist had two test subjects. They were the Sword Brothers. They were not killed. They were transported into his lab by the blast.

"I will find out if we can replicate their sword skills," he says to himself.

Outside…

"I'll take this thing apart one piece at a time!" Armor says to himself with determination.

The robot fires a flurry of small missiles at Armor. But with his high speed and flying skills, he evades them and makes them blow up by missing their mark.

Armor flies through one of the eyes of the robot, smashing through. Shards of thick glass fly inward, one large shard impaling a soldier.

"TIME TO AVENGE MY FRIENDS!" he yells in anger.

A soldier nervously says, "They're not dead…they were transported into this machine to be experimented on."

"Thanks!" Armor yells with gratitude as he throws the soldier through a nearby door.

He finds the lab and knocks on the door.

"Who would knock?" whispers the scientist as he opens the door.

Armor blows him away with a powerful blast.

"Time to get you boys out," he says as he frees his friends as they leave.

THE END

The Masters

Three men are in separate capsules. A professor stands at a console and enters a program. It programs their thoughts to try to stop evil. The three are now called the Masters.

In the capsules, there is a ninja, a samurai, and a young man named Joko. After being dressed and equipped, they are teleported to a warzone.

Standing in front of them are what appears to be zombie versions of themselves. Joko, holding a machine gun rifle, blows away the zombie version of himself as he yells, "You're not real!"

"Imposter!" says the samurai as he runs through the zombie samurai with his sword.

"Faker!" says the ninja as he slices away the zombie ninja with his blade.

Suddenly, the trio appears elsewhere, away from their fallen foes. Before them appears a small creature with a curly tail and a caped man with a bow and arrow.

The small creature spews slime all over Joko, causing him to groan in disgust.

The ninja flips in the air, slamming into the caped man. Then the ninja digs in with his small blades.

Elsewhere, a leader, aware of the three heroes, yells to his minion, "Get them!"

"Chill out!" says the heavily armed soldier back to his leader.

The soldier takes off in his helicopter. He tracks down the trio. He fires away, unleashing missiles and firing his machine gun. But they all miss their targets.

The ninja hurls three shuriken that hit their mark, causing the soldier to crash land.

Joko decides to take on the soldier. He charges forward, dodging the enemy's machine gun blasts. Joko kicks the soldier in the head. Simultaneously, Joko knees the soldier while the soldier punches Joko in the face. The soldier punches Joko again. Joko puts the soldier in a headlock, then handcuffs him. The three then tie him up, then decide to regroup by planning their next move and eating.

Unbeknownst to the Masters, the soldier has sent a homing signal to his leader. He then breaks out of his bindings and fights back. Joko kicks him in the face and the ninja slices his throat.

Joko sees that they have company. He tosses a gun to each of his comrades, saying "Someone's comin'! Take these!"

A large figure emerges, his hands glowing with power.

"Master sent me to kill you!" he growls menacingly.

Joko fires his gun, but the bullets bounces off the stranger's chest harmlessly. The stranger throws a small explosive which explodes at Joko's feet, sending him flying.

The stranger fires a blast from his hand at the ninja, who dodges, then leaps toward the stranger, sword first.

But the stranger vanishes, causing the ninja to fall and hit his head.

The samurai fires a blast from his gun, and it knocks the stranger down.

"Give up!" says the stranger to the samurai as he gets back up.

"No, thank you. I do not give up," says the samurai with conviction as he dives at the stranger but goes through him.

The stranger fires two blasts at the samurai, hitting him both times, sending him flying into a wall.

The samurai fires another blast, which hits the enemy in the head, killing him. The samurai grabs the stranger's necklace and cloak.

A vampire, a werewolf and a mummy emerge from the shadows and move swiftly to attack.

The samurai causes the mummy to disappear with his power. The ninja puts a silver bullet into his gun and quickly fires, killing the werewolf. Joko fired a stake into the vampire, killing him as well.

Suddenly an explosive hits Joko, killing him instantly. Three heavily armed and armored men come walking up.

"Your friend was an easy target," taunts one of the men.

The ninja leaps forward, but the leader grabs the ninja by the throat as he says, "Don't try anything on me, or you'll pay!"

He drops the ninja, who is now coughing.

The ninja and samurai are then captives and are taken elsewhere. The ninja is chained up and the samurai is encased in something that is supposed to weaken his magic.

When they are left alone, the samurai breaks out, and then releases the ninja. They sneak out.

They come across some guards, which the ninja takes out with his shuriken. The two change into uniforms.

They come across two more guards, one wearing a power pack. The samurai shoots the power pack, which explodes, vaporizing one guard and blowing off the legs of another.

A large floating creature appears, leading two guards. The creature is a large head with one eye.

"Freeze!" screams one of the guards threateningly.

The ninja and samurai raise their hands.

"Take them in," growls the creature.

"Get down when I shoot," the ninja whispers to the samurai.

BUDDA! BUDDA! Machine gun fire fills the air. As expected, the creature explodes, killing the two guards with its acidic blood.

The ninja and the samurai try to find their way out of the enemy stronghold.

But the enemy leader was able to track them down. The large, cloaked figure levitates menacingly toward the two fighters.

The ninja hurls a shuriken that hits the leader. With a groan of anger, he hurls off his cloak and whips out his sword. The ninja hurls a flurry of shuriken, hitting him. The samurai finishes off the leader with his sword.

The Masters find their way out and leave.

The End

Terminator X

Terminator X is a special forces soldier. He has high tech armor, a jetpack and a heavy machine gun.

He is flying and doing reconnaissance. Just as he is asking for his new orders, an enemy appears. He is flying with small jets at his sides. He is wearing a hood. He has a gun and a short sword.

"You won't be going anywhere after I'm done with you," the enemy laughingly says as he fires from his gun.

Terminator X dodges, but the bullet hits his jetpack, rendering it useless. He begins to plummet to the ground far below. As he is falling, he fires a grenade from his gun. The grenade flies and lodges into the enemy's chest. BOOM! Bits of remains fly in all directions.

Terminator X releases his parachute. It has a hole in it, so he falls more quickly.

He calls in to his boss, who is trying to locate him.

After he lands, an armored man with monstrous features charges toward him, raising a wrist blaster and bearing claws.

"DIE!" the stranger screams as he fires a blast.

Terminator X dodges, then fires a blast of his own. BRAP! Even with armor, the blasts rip the enemy apart.

Terminator X scans the landscape. He sees no civilization for miles. He then realizes that he is in the Desert of Death. He hangs tight for thirty minutes, then gets picked up…THE END

Strike!

Strike is a one-man army. He is a member of the special forces. He is a skilled fighter and a weapons specialist.

He is stealthily dropped into a combat zone where the battle is against alien monsters. He is doing recon when he sees some enemies within a short distance. He decides to get a better look, so he climbs onto a small building.

He sees that the aliens are developing a dangerous weapon, so he decides that he must stop them. He decides to take on a small group. He swings from a rope and punches one as he kicks another. He then pulls out his laser rifle and shoots four more.

One is getting close from behind. Strike fires his rifle. It hits a large nearby tree, which falls and crushes the creature flat.

He then hears an ear-piercing screech. He covers his ears. He then sees a dark figure before him, who is laughing in triumph.

Strike unleashes a barrage of blasts, hitting the figure in the face. Come to find out, it is a robot, the face appearing skeletal now after being blasted off. Strike fires more blasts, taking out the robot and a nearby alien in the process.

A small explosive hits him in the chest, knocking him back. An alien with a mullet stands before him, ready to attack. Strike connects with a jump kick, then punches the creature in the head. It screams with rage, then hurls Strike away.

The alien then transforms into a dog-like alien creature. It leaps at Strike, who dodges. Strike backhands the creature, then escapes while the creature is stunned…The End

Terak-Part 1

Terak is part of a special forces group. He is a soldier that typically fights alone.

He receives word that several hostile alien ships are heading toward his aircraft carrier. He gets in his jet and takes off, into battle. He shoots down two enemy ships.

He sees that he is in the enemy's sights. A split second before there is a direct hit, he slams the eject button, sending him out of the jet, through a massive explosion.

He drifts, dangling from his parachute for a second before he fires a grappling hook which attaches to an enemy ship, surprisingly unnoticed. Minutes later, the ships arrive back at their base, which is a massive robot. The pilot of the ship he was on gets out. Terak blasts the alien with his laser gun. The creature falls, smoke curling from its lifeless body. Terak throws his helmet off.

Outside, the base is being attacked by Terak's group.

Terak stealthily sneaks around, wanting to do some damage. A large-headed alien is muttering to itself as it approaches.

Utilizing his special technology, Terak presses a button on his wrist. Terak receives the power of fire as he is engulfed in flames. He fires a blast of flame into the enemy's face, killing it.

"Sorry, kid," Terak whispers as he changes back.

Continuing, Terak opens a small door. He sees his buddy, Joey, bloody and being carried by a large robot.

"Joey!" Terak yells reactively.

"QUARRY APPROACHING!" the robot says.

Terak carefully fires two blasts into the robots back. The robot falls and drops Joey. Terak runs over to his comrade.

"You okay, kid?" Terak says.

"Yeah," Joey mutters.

An armored reptilian creature appears, wielding a sword and a pike.

"Hiss...intruders!" it says, then mutters some special phrases, causing him to glow and armor up even more.

"Come with me," the reptile hisses.

"NO!" Joey yells defiantly.

The reptile fires blasts from his two bladed weapons. One encases Joey in a bubble and the other creates knockout gas in the bubble. Joey is out cold, floating in the bubble.

Terak fires a blast, destroying the creature's pike.

"Take this!" says Terak as he fires another blast.

BOOM! The reptile has deflected the blast with its sword.

"Obey human! Follow me!" it chants authoritatively.

"Am I stupid?" Terak asks as he fires again, destroying the reptile.

"Bang! Bang!" says Terak as he blows smoke from his gun barrel and walks past the carcass.

"Thanks!" Joey says as he is freed from the bubble.

A minute later, they come to a ladder. At the top, Terak peers out of the door at the top. He sees some guards. He throws a sleep grenade, sending them to sleep.

The duo proceeds. They come upon a power reactor. A nerdy man in a suit wields a large sword and stands before them.

"I'm the guard!" he says in a goofy voice.

"Face it, you're a wimp!" Joey says mockingly.

"Oh yeah?" he growls as he transforms into a monstrous creature.

He sends his clawed hand all the way through Joey, killing him.

"JOEY!" Terak shouts, "Nooo!"

He then fires three blasts into the creature, killing it in turn.

Terak then fires some blasts into the reactor, then quickly blasts out of the giant robot. He soars out, using his jetpack. Allied ships are attacking the base, firing blasts. The large structure explodes, sending Terak flying faster.

While flying over, he sees an ally attacking a tank. The tank destroys the ship, but the pilot ejects in time.

Terak hits a button on his wrist. Heavy metallic armor covers him. Terak falls into the tank, destroying it.

"Thanks!" says the pilot as Terak transforms back.

Two aliens are parachuting down from above. Terak destroys them with his blaster.

He sees two enemy ships coming toward them. He turns his blaster into a rocket and fires it at the two ships, destroying them in one shot.

Then, a large, monstrous, armored alien with clawed tentacles rises in front of the two men menacingly. One of the tentacles rips across Terak and picks him up. Terak blasts the tentacle with his blaster, severing it. He then blasts the creature in the head. Its body collapses in a heap.

"You're good…" says the other soldier.

But then, suddenly, the other soldier is stomped on & killed by a large robot.

Terak blasts into the foot of the giant machine, then sneaks inside. He comes upon three human guards and jumps into action. He destroys the armor of one with his blaster. He leaps through the air and lands on the head of another. The third throws a grenade, but misses, the explosion rocking the room.

Terak switches on a chainsaw knife and decapitates one, then stabs another in the chest. He throws the knife at the last one, hitting him in the chest and killing him.

Terak eventually ends up near the command center. There is an eerie presence. Four supernatural and monstrous creatures appear.

One appears to have some type of death touch. As it swings to touch Terak, Terak jumps in the air above, causing the demon to touch its own face. Terak finishes it off by slamming down from above with both feet.

Terak slams another demon with a simultaneous punch and kick, causing the demon to stumble hard into a pillar. The pillar falls and crushes one of the other demons.

Terak kicks another in the stomach, then he clicks a button on his wrist, giving him armor with spikes. Terak punches clean through the creature.

The last demon screeches defiantly. Terak backhands the creature, then sinks into the shadows. The remaining demon stumbles in the dark, searching in vain. Terak ends up behind it and taps it on the shoulder. Terak slams it with a punch to the face.

Terak then blasts into the ceiling. Debris starts to fall. He fires into the nearby wall as he smashes through it. Seconds later, the giant machine explodes. Terak flies back to his base.

Part 2

Terak stands before his superiors.

"We have a new mission for you," the head of the group says as he shows a new enemy on the screen. "This is Modack. He is a great fighter. He has many warriors. You must stop him. My super squad will assist you."

Terak and his men approach the base. Terak shows off his powers as he flies with the wind. The men have special backpacks.

Suddenly as they stand ready to approach, one of the men is hit in the chest by a blast and dies.

A lone cyborg stands atop the base. He fires a missile. Terak changes into a solid steel form just in time as the missile hits the group of men, killing all but Terak.

The cyborg keeps firing his weapons at Terak, but to no effect as he calmly marches toward him. Terak slaps the cyborg's weapon out of his hand.

"I am Destructus. I will help you defeat Modack!" he says pleadingly. "I was one of his cyborgs. He has a large army."

He gives Terak a detonator. They distance themselves from the base, then set it off. The explosion rocks the air and ground all around them and debris fly in all directions.

A minute later, Modack flies toward them.

"You traitor!" howls Modack to the cyborg.

Terak fires a blast, hitting Modack in the chest and causing him to crash into the ground. Terak puts Modack in a headlock.

They take Modack back to their base for interrogation and imprisonment.

The End

Phase: The Threat of Monsters

Which are stronger, men or monsters?

Phase is a soldier. He is part of a team that is trying to stop monsters from taking over the world. He has high-tech weapons. He has a motorcycle, a submarine and a few airplanes.

He arrives at his base. Enemy ships begin to attack. He and three others in his squad (Wildcat, Radicool, & Ol' Cat) are in vehicles called mechs that are fighter jets that also change into robots.

There is such an enormous army attacking, that they decide to split up so that the enemy cannot destroy them in one attack if the three of them are grouped together.

<u>Wildcat-</u>Wildcat breaks into an enemy ship. An enemy soldier fires at him, but the blast bounces off his armor. Wildcat fires a blast from his visor, vaporizing the soldier. He then blasts out of the ship. It crashes shortly after. Another enemy ship approaches. It completes a direct hit on his mech. With his armor damaged severely, he is now exposed and vulnerable.

<u>Radicool-</u>Elsewhere, Radicool attacks an enemy soldier with his bladed wings, slicing off the soldier's hand, causing the soldier to screech in agony.

Three enemies approach from behind. The leader is also armored with wings. Another enemy is cloaked and has a mask. The last is winged as well, looking like a bat.

"We are the Eagles!" announces the leader.

Radicool evades them, seeing how he is outnumbered. But they follow. He fires behind and misses the trio but hits and destroys an enemy ship.

Finding a better position, Radicool fires at the bat-like enemy, hitting him in the face and the wings, causing him to crash and explode.

The cloaked figure fires a barrage of blasts from his hands, causing Radicool to drop his gun and barely dodge. Radicool punches him in the face. The leader fires and misses Radicool. Radicool kicks the leader in the face. The leader falls hard, triggering a grenade.

"Noooo!" scream the leader and Radicool simultaneously.

BOOM! All are reduced to bits.

<u>Ol' Cat-</u> Ol' Cat wields a power sword, glowing with energy. Two larger ships approach. One grabs him and pulls him

in. He stealthily enters the hangar bay in the ship. He finds a soldier fueling a jet. Ol' Cat runs him through with his sword, then puts on the enemy uniform.

Shortly after, another soldier closely approaches.

"Hey, I heard a…" the soldier says.

Ol' Cat swiftly stabs the soldier in the chest.

"…noise," the soldier gasps as he dies, the sword running him through.

Ol' Cat quickly enters the ship and fires into the reactor core with a short blast. He then quickly leaves the larger ship, which erupts in an explosion seconds later. He returns to the base.

<u>Phase</u>-Phase's mech is being attacked by two robots. He changes into a jet and flies upward, then jets downward, firing a hail of blasts which destroy the attacking bots.

Seconds later, he finds two other comrades from his force. But all three of them get shot down. As they descend with their parachutes, they see an armored man, glowing with power and he is laughing.

The trio fire their heavy machine guns at the villain, but the bullets bounce off the villain's forcefield.

"Don't give up!" Phase shouts over the blasts. "We have to make it wear off!"

Suddenly, the force field evaporates. Phase tosses a grenade. BOOM! The villain is stumbling and weakened. Smoke drifts from his armor. Phase extends claws from his gloves as he charges toward the enemy. He slices into the villain's chest. Phase punches him in the face, then throws him down. Hard.

"You are powerful…" the villain mutters, then vanishes in a puff of smoke.

Machine gun blasts fill the air as a tiger-faced enemy ship approaches. Phase and one of the others take cover.

"Save yourselves! Kill them!" the other yells as he stands defiantly. He is hit multiple times and dies.

The other remaining soldier yells, "Take this!" as he fires away with his heavy machine gun, hitting the ship hundreds of times, causing the ship to crash land.

Phase enters the ship and finishes off the enemies inside.

Phase is then able to call for reinforcements. His team brings a ship that closely resembles the one that they brought down. Phase receives coordinates for his next target. It is King Ti-Ara's hideout. It is an Egyptian tomb. It is disguised on the outside as a giant funhouse.

Inside, King Ti-Ara is in his chambers with some of his henchmen. A prisoner is chained to the wall. The king sees on his surveillance screen that Phase is coming for him. He laughs with glee.

Outside, Phase's small ship approaches the entrance, which is a clown face. In the mouth, stands a giant clown. But Phase shoots him down, the clown laughing as he falls. Upon entering, the ship is attacked by several giant flame monsters that look like dinosaurs. After destroying several with his blasters, Phase finds an entrance to the inside. It is too small for his ship, so he lands and enters.

An Egyptian approaches, glowing with power and carrying an Ankh.

"Go no further!" bellows the Egyptian, menacingly. He blasts Phase with his power, causing Phase to groan in pain.

Suddenly, the Egyptian is punched from behind by a stranger, the impact throwing him several feet.

"Are you okay?" the stranger says to Phase. "I'm Metallius."

Metallius is cloaked and has a mask. He also carries a bow and quiver.

Groaning, the Egyptian throws his ankh. It glows and transforms into a large, menacing hulk of a man.

"He did this!" Phase yells as he blasts the Egyptian in the chest with his machine gun.

"This will fix him!" says Metallius as he launches an explosive arrow at the large figure.

The arrow only makes the creature stronger. He laughs as the blast gives him power and causes him to grow larger, grow fangs and sharp teeth.

Phase fires his machine gun, but the demon's power just continues to absorb the bullets. The demon cackles at the feeble attempt.

"YOU'RE JUST GIVING ME MORE POWER!" it growls. It then grabs Phase by the wrists and electrocutes him with its growing power.

Metallius punches the creature in the face. The creature grabs Metallius in a bear hug and squeezes, causing Metallius to groan in pain. Metallius punches the creature again, causing the creature to let go of him. Metallius launches a power arrow at the creature.

"No...too much power!" it mutters as it starts glowing brighter and brighter.

Phase and Metallius dive for cover seconds before the creature explodes.

The heroic duo venture further into the caves. They hear rhythmic chanting. They peer through an entrance into a large cavern. They see a large statue down below. A cloaked figure is wielding a dagger and is about to sacrifice a man that is tied to an altar.

Metallius launches an arrow, hitting the cloaked man in the shoulder, causing him to drop the dagger.

"Augh!" the cloaked man exclaims. "Kill them!" he screams to his followers.

The tied-up man miraculously grabbed the dagger in the air as it fell. He cuts himself free.

"I'm Strato. Help!" he yells as he runs up the stairs toward Phase and Metallius, the crowd following him with spears.

Phase and Metallius hear something from behind as they are about to act. A guard with a bug face and a large gun spots them.

Strato says, "I'd rather be speared than shot!" he says as he turns and runs toward the crowd and fires from a wrist blaster. He starts fighting like a madman, kicking and slashing with the dagger.

After making short work of the guard, Phase and Metallius join Strato in the fight. Phase blasts with his machine gun. Metallius mostly uses his fists. The three fight back to back.

Minutes later, Phase, who is normally unfazed by violence, is nauseated by the carnage that surrounds them.

Suddenly, the trio sees movement. The large statue has come to life, seeing so much bloodshed before it. It decides it wants more. It leaps toward Phase and slams the floor with its fists, barely missing Phase as he jumped out of the way.

"Eat this!" yells Phase as he tosses a grenade, blowing up a lot of the face of the giant. "Have some more!" he says as he then throws three more grenades.

The giant statue is reduced to rubble.

In a nearby room, they find clothing and armor. Phase puts on some durable armor that includes bracers that can fire blasts. Metallius finds a black suit with a pair of long daggers. Strato puts on an exoskeleton that has a jetpack and claws.

Nearby, they find three doors. They decide to split up.

<u>Phase</u>-Phase hears a cry for help through a nearby wall. He smashes through and frees the man, who suddenly vanishes. He then

sees glowing eyes and fangs in the dark. A vampire beast materializes in front of him. It blasts with its eyes, but Phase blocks the blast with his bracers.

Phase slams the vampire in the face, then blasts him with his bracers. The vampire lays prone on the floor, smoke billowing from its body. Phase enters a door in front of him.

"No!" he yells.

Metallius-As Metallius enters his door, unbeknownst to him, he is being watched on a surveillance screen. Minutes later, he sees guards coming at him from behind, wielding large blasters. He smashes through a door. He sees a chute in the floor, then jumps in. He slides down hundreds of feet, then falls into another hole.

Strato-As Strato enters his door, he sees an enemy. Strato shocks him violently. He enters the next door in front of him. Two enemies stand before him. A muscular mummy and an armored, winged soldier.

The mummy swings at Strato and the armored soldier fires a blast from his hands. Strato dodges and the blast hits the mummy. But the blast gives the mummy nuclear power. The mummy growls as it slams the ground near Strato and sends him flying.

Strato blasts the mummy with his visor. It overcharges the mummy's power.

"Too much power!" it growls, then explodes.

Strato gets hit by a blast from the armored soldier, which knocks him down.

Groaning, Strato drags himself to his feet, smoke billowing from his armor. Strato quickly hurls a sword at the enemy and it is buried up to the hilt in the armored soldier.

With his armor being destroyed from the blast, he puts on the winged armor of the soldier.

Three figures materialize out of the shadows. An armored man with blades coming out of his bracelets, a large muscular man, and a Cyborg. They approach menacingly.

Phase-A large figure crouches before Phase. He wears a helmet and there is a fist design on his chest. He holds a handgun and a combination of a sword and a morning star (like a mace, yet the ball and spikes are attached to a chain that is attached to the hilt of the sword).

Phase blasts from his helmet, which hits his foe in the helmet.

The enemy hurls the combo weapon at Phase. Phase dodges, then the weapon explodes upon hitting a wall. A blast from his gun is deflected by Phase's bracers. The enemy grunts as Phase kicks him in the face with both feet. Phase is thrown by the impact when the adversary slams the ground. Phase's claws come out. He slashes the opponent in the chest, causing him to drop his gun. The enemy fires a blast from his eyes, hitting Phase in the chest.

"Okay, you asked for it!" Phase groans loudly. He punches his enemy, causing him to fly across the room. Then Phase blasts him in the chest with his helmet blaster.

In the next room, there is a pool that leads to another area. He puts on his scuba gear. He sees three armored enemies who want to get him. Reacting quickly, Phase rips through the leader's breathing apparatus. The two others fire at him with their underwater blasters but miss.

<u>Metallius-</u>Metallius yells as he falls. Quickly, he fires an arrow with a grappling hook on it that is attached to a very fine but extremely strong cable. He connects with the ceiling outside of the hole and pulls himself up. As he does so, he looks down to see a corpse impaled on spikes below.

On the other side of the pit that he fell into, he sees a hole and enters it. As he emerges, he is attacked by an enemy, losing his bow and quiver. During the scuffle, he missteps and falls into yet another hole, but his cape gets caught on the way down, slowing down his momentum. He luckily grabs a handhold. He finds a cave near the handhold.

After seemingly hours, he finds a place to rest. He finds a small animal and enjoys a small meal over a fire. Minutes later, as he ventures away, he ambushes a guard and stabs him. Then he puts on the uniform.

An armored enemy figure approaches and sees through the disguise. He swings a morning star at the head of Metallius.

<u>Strato-</u>Strato blasts the head of the cyborg with the visor of his helmet. He hurls a short sword at the armored enemy, hitting him in the upper ribs.

"Take this!" the armored enemy says as he fires blades at Strato. He misses. "Tough guy, eh?" he continues.

Strato punches the armored man in the chest, then blasts him and the muscular man with energy blasts. He fires an energy blast and then a small missile into the trio, causing a small explosion.

***

Strato, Phase, and Metallius get in contact with their radios. They meet up after homing in on one another. They enter the hangar of the enemy and get in powerful ships. They use bombs and rockets to destroy the base.

The End!

Strato-Part 1

Strato is part of a special defense group that protects his planet against evil. He wears a black leather uniform and wears a trademark scarf. He has superhuman strength, enhanced senses, as well as excellent fighting abilities. He receives word that enemies are approaching his base. He jumps into his ship and heads toward the enemy.

With an enemy ship in his sights, he destroys it with one shot. Another enemy ship approaches, shaped like a head. It fires first and damages one of the wings of his ship. But he fires everything he has at the ship and destroys it.

He is forced to crash land. Luckily, he does so safely. Another fortunate thing happens. He ends up near an allied camp. The commanding officer, Torgo, knows Strato and is grateful to have his help. They are fighting against the enemy, both sides in trenches.

Suddenly, a massive and powerful being emerges from the enemy camp. As he struts toward the allied trenches, the allied forces fire at him. The bullets bounce off harmlessly.

"Go get him!" Torgo says to Strato.

Without hesitation, Strato courageously runs to the giant. Strato leaps and kicks his enemy in the face.

The giant's head is thrown back and he groans. Strato backhands the giant. The giant fires a blast from his hand and hits Strato, causing him to grunt in pain. A blast hits the giant in the back. The giant turns to see an armored, winged soldier carrying a blaster, smoke now drifting from it.

The giant fires a blast from his eyes, knocking down the other soldier.

Strato fires a blast from his laser rifle while Torgo fires a blast from a bazooka simultaneously. Finally, the giant falls with a crash.

Then, the allies hear several enemy ships approaching. The ships are shaped like tigers.

The allies unleash all their firepower, taking out several enemy ships.

The armored soldier grabs Strato & Torgo and flies to another spot. The trio take out enemy soldiers as they go.

"Everyone out! Quick!" the commanding officer yells anxiously.

Seconds later, there is a massive explosion, throwing soldiers in every direction.

The soldiers on both sides regroup and reload.

Gunfire and explosions break out. Soldiers are blown apart. Shots rain down from ships above. Rockets fire on both sides, destroying some of the ships above.

Torgo unleashes some claws and rips through another soldier.

An ally helicopter dangles a rope ladder and the remaining allies get in the helicopter. It takes off. Their new assignment is at an enemy base.

Strato, Torgo, and another soldier enter through the front. Then three more go around on each side.

The main trio breaks the door down. The other soldier ambitiously steps forward. He sets off a tripwire. Three spikes enter his chest, killing him instantly. A giant spiked ball descends from down the hall and is heading toward the others. Torgo destroys it with a blast from his gun.

Torgo falls into a pit but flies out. Three enemies emerge from the shadows menacingly.

Meanwhile, outside, one soldier sets off a trap where a giant log smashes him. Another soldier with him is caught in a trap, then devoured by a wild beast. The third of that group is caught in a net, then devoured by primitive cannibals.

The three on the other side fall into a pit with spikes at the bottom.

Back inside, Torgo squares off against a massive cyclops. A blast from its eye destroys Torgo's helmet. Torgo fires a blast from his gun, killing the enemy. A tiger-like beast man destroys his gun with flame from his mouth. The third enemy, a samurai, throws a flurry of shuriken, which destroy Torgo's armor. Torgo lets out two powerful blasts from his wrist blaster and kills the two remaining enemies.

Strato and Torgo stand amidst the smoke. Four ninjas materialize into view, surrounding them. One quickly destroys Torgo's wrist blaster.

Strato leaps into action. He punches one ninja in the face, then kicks two others at the same time, each one hit by a kick. He then punches the other ninja. The ninjas are out cold. Strato sheds some layers, removing his jacket, goggles and scarf.

Two sword welding enemies emerge. Strato takes them out quickly with his laser rifle. Strato and Torgo grab the blades of the fallen enemies.

The two of them then come upon a large assembly hall. A man is about to be sacrificed on an altar. Dozens of men are watching the dark festivities.

The priest suddenly finds a short sword in his back, thrown by Strato.

"Get them!" the priest groans with his dying breath.

The captive breaks out, then picks up the short sword and the dagger that the priest had. An onlooker approaches him with a spear. The captive stabs the spearman with his short sword. The captive then throws the spear which hits a ninja that was in a cave up above, that was ready to fire an arrow.

"I'm Lakro," says the former captive.

Strato, Torgo, and Lakro fight ferociously for their lives. Blades flying, blood splattering.

Minutes later, a masked, armored man wielding a shield and a Morningstar yells, "STOP!"

Lakro kicks the enemy, but then the enemy strikes him with his shield. The enemy then chokes Strato, who stabs him. The enemy then lets go. Torgo throws a dagger, which enters the enemy's head. He falls.

The trio continues onward. A massive, imposing monster of a man appears. Strato slices across his chest but is backhanded away. The trio attack, but all their blades are broken over the man. The trio then offer him to join them. He agrees.

"I am Rage," he says. "I have been fighting on the wrong side."

A hairy robed man approaches. He fires a blast from his hands, which Strato deflects with one of his swords. Strato kicks the man in the face, then stabs him in the heart.

A cyborg on a motorcycle fires at them. Strato takes him out with his blades. Another enemy attacks with a club, hitting Strato in the face. Strato slices across the enemy's chest. The enemy misses with his club, then grabs Strato's face.

Yards away, Rage fights another massive man. They swing, hit, and kick each other. Rage finally takes out the enemy. He hears something. Around a corner, he sees some robots. Rage punches one, who drops its blaster. The robots copy his face, which infuriates him. He then picks up the blaster and blows the three robots away.

He hears something and ducks barely in time. BOOM! A massive fist slams the wall near him.

"You are finished, human! You can't survive against the power of Vormov!" a massive armored monster growls.

Yards away, Lakro finishes off a ninja. A football hits him in the chest. A group of huge, angry football players approach. He hurls the football at the group with all his might at them, which knocks them over.

The football players are then crushed by giant robot basketball players. One tries to stomp on Lakro, but he jumps out of the way. Lakro is then picked up. Lakro slashes away with his blades at the hand that grabbed him. It drops him, but then he lands in a net.

A man dressed in sports gear appears and says, "Hello. I'm Sportsmaster. Watch this."

He tosses a sphere into the group of basketball players and creates a force field around him and Lakro.

BOOM! A massive explosion rocks the ground, sending debris in all directions. Sportsmaster cackles.

Lakro decides that Sportsmaster is crazy, so he lunges at him with his blades. But Sportsmaster fires a blast from his spiked bat, sending Lakro flying onto an ice rink. Sword-wielding robotic hockey players surround Lakro, who has begun to slide around. Lakro slashes and destroys one, which explodes.

Meanwhile, Torgo chokes an armored soldier, then punches him, sending him flying. The enemy then fires at Torgo with his handguns, grazing Torgo's sides. A blast from the enemy's helmet hits Torgo in the chest. Then the enemy fires rockets from his shoulders, which explode and send Torgo flying. Torgo groans and isn't getting up. The enemy puts his foot on Torgo's chest and laughs hysterically.

Torgo musters his strength and swings then connects after clasping his hands together, sending the enemy flying. The enemy dies upon impact after hitting the wall. Hard.

Torgo then gets shocked from behind. Four enemies in uniforms stand behind him. He grabs the enemy that shocked him by the wrists and forces him to shock two of the others, the other one dodging. Torgo then uses incredible strength to punch through the shocking enemy. The last of the four shocks him.

Elsewhere, Strato slashes his enemy across the chest, killing him. A dark figure emerges out of the shadows.

"Impressive," the man says.

Untrusting the stranger, Strato kicks him.

"You shouldn't have done that," growls the stranger as he transforms into a werewolf and rips out of his clothing.

Strato slices across the werewolf's face, then knees him. He then sends a flurry of punches into his face. The werewolf falls as he changes back into a man.

"I must find the others!" Strato says with determination.

He finds Vormov looming over Rage. Strato whips out his blades and slashes the back of the monster's head as Rage fires a blast into the creature's face.

Vormov turns and growls, "Who are you?"

"Your executioner!" yells Strato as he slices across the creature's face.

Vormov backhands Strato, then fires a stun blast from his wrist, knocking Strato out.

Rage and Vormov fire at each other simultaneously. Rage hits Vormov in the chest while Vormov misses. Rage kicks across Vormov's chest, then unleashes a flood of punches into the creature's face.

Strato has then recovered. He finishes off the creature with a deep slash to the chest.

Strato then finds Torgo through his keen senses. Just as Strato is ready to attack, the enemy with supernatural ability blasts outward from his body, knocking Strato & Torgo back. The enemy then picks up the two with his power, while shocking them.

Suddenly, a shuriken and a gun blast bounce off the enemy.

Three figures come into view. One is a hooded, mystical being named Claw. The second is a masked and well-armed man named Greystarr. The third is like a ninja, named White Ghost.

Surrender!" Greystarr says to the enemy.

Claw then envelopes the enemy in his cloak.

"No! I can't be beat…" he groans and then is vaporized.

The three newcomers help Rage, Strato and Torgo recover.

"Get our friend," says Rage.

The cloaked figure finds Lakro, who had been knocked out by an explosion after destroying the robots.

Claw revives the captive.

"Who are you?" Lakro says.

"A friend," says Claw.

"Of who?" says Lakro.

"Strato, Torgo, and Rage," Claw says. "Come," he continues as he transforms into a large bird and carries Lakro back to the others.

Then, Sportsmaster appears and says, "Stop! Come with me!"

"NO!" says Greystarr as he fires a blast, which hits a bomb that was in Sportsmaster's hand.

It explodes and knocks Sportsmaster back. Sportsmaster's armor is shredded and smoke curls from his body, but he is alive. He swings with his club at Greystarr, but Greystarr blocks the attack with his knife.

Sportsmaster then drops the club and extends some claws.

"A challenge!" Strato pipes up as he engages with Sportsmaster with his blades.

They fight ferociously, but in the end, Strato slices through him with his blades.

They then call a ship to come and get them. Thirty minutes later, they are picked up.

Epilogue

Back at Strato's base, his superior is meeting with the seven of them.

"I would like the six of you to join Strato in a mission. I will give you new suits, weapons, and equipment," says the leader.

Strato has a speed suit. Torgo has more firepower. Claw has a power stone. Greystarr has a heavy machine gun. White Ghost is now White Spirit and has a shape-changing suit. Rage now combines his brute strength with a sharp blade. Lakro is now the master of disguise.

All but Strato and White Spirit were riding in a transport, speeding to the mission. Strato was running in his speed suit and White Spirit was flying.

Suddenly, a bomb is dropped from above, destroying the car. As Strato & White Spirit are surveying the damage, the ship that attacked, lands nearby.

"I killed them!" says a man in a cloak and a hockey mask.

White Spirit changes into a demon and Strato runs over, unleashing a flurry of punches. The stranger zaps Strato, killing him. White Spirit shoves a giant pincer through the enemy, then lifts him. White Spirit scavenges supplies and weapons from the wreckage. He sees an enemy car and a motorcycle coming toward him. He fires an Uzi in each hand, destroying the vehicles.

He then gets back to base to regroup.

The End

Nemesis

Nemesis is a heavily muscled vigilante who specializes in heavy firepower.

One of his enemies is a crazed scientist in California. The scientist has created a genetically mutated dinosaur: the brontoceratodinolestes. The creature is intelligent. The scientist has the creature track down Nemesis, who is in Mexico.

The dinosaur catches Nemesis off guard and takes him to the scientist. Nemesis breaks free and punches the scientist.

"Get him!" says the scientist to a nearby henchman.

The henchman has a knife and a gun. The henchman stops a punch from Nemesis, who then knocks the knife out of his hand. The henchman fires his gun, but Nemesis dodges and slams into some chemicals, then gets shocked by the scientist's equipment.

The combination of the chemicals and the shock cause a reaction in Nemesis, which strengthens and infuriates him. With renewed fervor, he charges toward the scientist.

"Get in the blaster!" the scientist screams in desperation, referring to a weaponized car.

"Okay!" says the henchman as he runs to the vehicle.

"C'mere, punk!" yells Nemesis as he grabs the scientist by the coat and lifts him.

BLAM! BRAP! Bullets slam the floor near Nemesis, who then throws the scientist.

The henchman fires again, hitting Nemesis in the chest, only making him angrier. Nemesis picks up the car and throws it.

Another henchman comes. Nemesis uppercuts him. Nemesis is pummeling the henchman to a pulp when he hears loud stomping and roaring. The dinosaur is back.

The scientist desperately tries to control it with his remote, but the dragon does not respond. It breathes fire at the scientist, who dodges the flames.

Nemesis hurls a grenade at the creature. It explodes. Chunks of flesh, bone, and blood fly in all directions.

"Why?" Nemesis yells as grabs and shakes the scientist.

"I wanted to make the most…" says the scientist but is cut off mid-sentence by a screeching pterodactyl as it digs into his head from above, causing the scientist to scream in pain.

Nemesis hurls a dagger, which finds its mark by digging into the creature's skull and entering its small brain, killing it. Nemesis quickly fires into the machinery and scientific equipment. There is sparking, then the lab begins to burn.

Nemesis leaves quickly.

Part 2

Later, Nemesis makes it back to the city and is in street clothes.

He comes across a hostage situation. A masked man is holding a gun to young woman's head.

While the kidnapper is distracted by the police, Nemesis kicks the gun out of the man's hand.

"Get outta here!" yells Nemesis.

"Next time, old man!" he yells as he runs and evades the police.

Amazingly, the police do not give Nemesis a hard time. The girl gives him a hug, then he leaves.

Elsewhere, a group of villains plot to take out Nemesis.

A robed, bearded figure steps out of the shadows and says, "I'll get him," as electricity crackles from his hands.

Later, the group finds Nemesis on the streets, although he is incognito.

"You're going down!" says the bearded man as he sucker-punches Nemesis, who then evades the group.

Nemesis enters a diner and changes into his battle gear. He kicks the door open and enters the street, firing blasts from his Uzi into one of his attackers, a cloaked man with a necklace.

Another attacker, appearing like a demon, charges forward, but Nemesis blows him away too.

The one who punched him hurls a fierce lightning bolt, which destroys the Uzi. Nemesis hurls back a grenade, which blows that enemy apart.

The kidnapper returns. He shoots at Nemesis, who dodges, then kicks up into the man's face, knocking him backward.

The kidnapper punches Nemesis, knocking him down. He thrusts his gun and points it at Nemesis as he looms over him.

"You'll never get away with…this!" Nemesis says as he kicks up and knocks the gun out of his enemy's hand.

Nemesis gets up and gives the man a one two punch, knocking him down.

It is then Nemesis's turn to thrust his gun at his enemy. He pulls the trigger.

Click. The barrel was empty. He takes the villain to jail.
The End

Energy

Energy is a one-man wrecking crew. With his power, he can fire blasts from his hands and fly at high speeds. He also has superhuman strength. He also has a powerful sword.

He receives word of a ten-story robot attacking the city. He flies past several buildings and comes upon the giant machine. It tries to grab him. With his sword, he slashes off its thumb and forefinger. He then slams the head with a powerful punch, knocking it back.

He then slams into the head of the robot and breaks into it. He catches a few soldiers by surprise. He backhands one, knocking him out and sending his helmet flying. Another grabs him from behind by the neck. He sends a blast outward and knocks the soldier back.

He then comes upon two soldiers guarding the pilot. He sends a massive blast, destroying the face of the robot from the inside, sending pieces of metal flying outward, along with the three soldiers.

The massive machine falls as Energy flies away.

THE END

BOLTS!

The Bolts are a trio of martial arts masters. They are Darkbolt, Bolt Blade, and White Flash. They rid the world of demons and other evils that prey on the innocent.

While traveling through a mountainous valley, the Bolts see some ferocious demons approaching. The demons are drooling with hunger. The fighters clasp their weapons tightly, ready to fight. Kojima, the leader of the Demons, brandishes his sword and tells his minions to charge the three heroes. The Demons also pull out their weapons and close in on the heroes.

Darkbolt hurls a Chinese star at a demon with the head of a squid. The star gets imbedded into its head. The creature screams in pain and falls to the ground. A demon with its mouth stitched together has leaped off a nearby cliff overhead. It grasps a dagger in one of its clawed hands. White Flash swiftly grabs the demon and throws him into the leader.

Bolt Blade lets out a fierce battle cry and leaps into the air toward the drooling monster. The monster screams with glee. The monster's blade grazes Bolt Blade's arm. Bolt Blade quickly chops the demon's head off.

Kojima leaps to his feet and one of his demons stumbles to its feet beside him. Darkbolt hurls his Sai at the minion. The Sai goes through its mouth and comes out of the back of its head. Darkbolt and Bolt Blade pull out their swords from their backs and get ready to fight.

"After I defeat you, you will fear me…that is if you are still alive!" bellows Kojima.

Darkbolt swiftly leaps toward the enemy, leading with his sword. With two swift movements of his sword, Kojima slices Dark Bolt's mask off and slices one of Bolt Blade's swords in half. He then vanishes in a large puff of smoke…THE END…FOR NOW

Battle Crew

Battle Crew is a group of nine heroes. They are checking things out in the world and see something going on in Frog City. The main building is shaped like a giant frog. They see on their surveillance that the building is changing, and it has become an evil city after it has been conquered by an evil army.

The nine heroes teleport there. They see that there are three different entrances, so they decide to split up into three groups of three.

Cool/Mohawk/Blizzard-Mohawk and Cool are heavily armed. Blizzard has power over cold.

They hear something. It is a lizard-like creature with a mace.

"It's a tunnel gleech! Get him no matter the costs!" Mohawk says as he cocks his machine gun.

He fires and misses. The creature chants in an alien language, then delivers a glancing blow across Mohawk's chest. Mohawk blasts the mace out of the creature's hand.

Blizzard and Cool square off against it, Cool with a dagger. Blizzard swings and the creature vanishes, causing Blizzard to punch Cool in the face.

"Sorry, man!" Blizzard says.

"It's okay! Don't do it again," says Cool.

Cool whips out his machine gun and blows away the creature.

They enter the next room, which appears like a bedroom.

Suddenly, a small explosive detonates near Cool, sending him flying.

A large man in a suit resembling that of a porcupine tosses a chair, hitting Mohawk and knocking him back. Mohawk fires from his machine gun, but it doesn't seem to slow the large man down. The porcupine man punches Mohawk. Blizzard then freezes the man solid.

"Blast! I'll get them myself!" an armored man yells angrily as he enters the room, gun in hand.

Cloak/X/Skull-Cloak has a cloak on, X has a suit covered in X's, and Skull has a skull mask.

As they enter their door, three masked men approach.

"Go no further!" says the middle figure.

Then, the three pull out their blades menacingly. One fires a blast from his sword, but X blocks it with his power, which overpowers the masked man's power and eventually takes him out.

Cloak is fighting another masked man and gets slashed across the back. In a flash of power, his cloak is vaporized and he uppercuts his enemy, knocking him out. He then puts the enemy's mask on.

Skull fires small rockets from his wrist, blowing up the last masked man.

Mask/Streek/Rad-Mask is armored. Streek is plain-looking other than his visor. Rad is also dressed plainly but wears a mask.

"I sense danger!" Mask says, seconds before a large demon appears in front of them.

"Move!" says Mask just as a blast from the demon hits him, light shooting out of his eye sockets.

Streek fires with his visor, which causes the demon to shrink down to human size. He then fires a blast from his fingers, which blast off the enemy's horns.

The demon punches Streek. Rad hits the demon with a mental blast, then roundhouse kicks it. The demon fires back from his eyes, hitting Rad.

Mask punches the demon, then plunges his sword through the creature.

Suddenly, with a burst of flame, a man stands before them.

"Who are you?" he calmly demands.

Cool/Mohawk/Blizzard-"Freeze!" demands the armored man.

Blizzard hits the man with a burst of cold, causing him to drop his gun. The man reaches to grab another gun, but Cool fires a gun of his own, the blast entering through the man's heart. His dead body hits the floor.

An alien robot monster emerges from the shadows. Mohawk blasts it with his gun.

Cloak/X/Skull-An armored man, a muscular man, and a man in a large machine that has heavy machine guns run into the room.

All three heroes attack, killing all three with one shot.

Skull sees a remote near the TV.

"No! Don't!" X says.

But he is too late. Skull pushes the button and his armor is blown off.

X removes his mask.

Suddenly, a man in black emerges from the floor with a laugh.

"C'mon! Anyone!" he says, beckoning with a clawed finger.

X swings at him, but he grabs X by the wrist and slams him down.

The stranger claws across Skulls and Cloak's chest simultaneously. Then Skull dies after the stranger rips out Skull's heart. X quickly grabs Skull's missile bracelets.

Cloak begins to glow with power. He grabs the stranger and shocks him. Then the stranger is punched in the face by a giant toad, wielding spiked brass knuckles. The stranger falls to the floor, lifeless.

"Mr. Toad!" exclaims Cloak.

Mr. Toad joins the group.

Mask/Streek/Rad-"We're Battle Crew!" says Mask.

"I am Flaming Knight," says the man. "May I join you? I know of the evil that is here."

Flaming Knight joins them, and they continue.

Suddenly, Mask and Streek are shot from behind. They die instantly.

Flame Knight envelops the assassin in flame with his power. The killer flails around until he collapses. Nothing but charred bones remain.

Flame Knight puts on Streek's visor and Mask's armor. They continue.

Unfortunately, due to the weight of the armor, Flame Knight falls through the floor and into lava.

Fortunately, the armor protects him until he can create a force field that protects him more. He strips off the armor.

Meanwhile, Rad sees a motorcycle coming toward him. It then changes into a robot. Two armored soldiers are at its sides. One of them hits Rad with his nun chucks.

The three enemies fire at Rad simultaneously, but Rad blocks the attacks with his power and deflects the bullets back at the enemies, killing them all.

Rad then puts on the armor of one of the soldiers. Rad is then hit in the side of the head by a flying fist.

Meanwhile, Flame Knight tries to emerge from the lava, but is having a hard time. The shield springs a leak and some lava splashes on him.

He yells with determination and blasts out of the pit. He appears near Rad, who identifies himself, then blasts the robot who had hit him with the flying fist.

Flame Knight and Rad decide to leave and go home.

Cool/Mohawk/Blizzard-Blizzard fires an extreme blast of cold, finishing off the creature. Things start to get warm, so Mohawk sheds his mask and Cool sheds his leather jacket.

A zombie emerges from the shadows. Mohawk and Cool blast it. It explodes.

An orb floats toward them. Cool grabs it and presses a button on it. It teleports them outside. They head back to their base.

Cloak/X/Mr. Toad-A winged demon appears and destroys Mr. Toad's brass knuckles. Mr. Toad whips out his six shooters and empties the guns by firing at the creature. No effect.

Mr. Toad unleashes his tongue and grabs the creature, then kicks it in the face. He tightens his tongue until the creature dies.

The heroes continue. Then a large, muscular creature rumbles toward them. He fights Mr. Toad. They punch at the same time and slam fists. Twice. It fires a blast from its hand but misses Mr. Toad. Mr. Toad punches the creature in the face, then wraps his tongue around the creature. The creature breaks free.

"My tongue!" Mr. Toad says, sounding muffled, then punches the creature in the jaw.

Cloak and X fire away with their powers and destroy the creature.

The trio leaves the building. Frog City is then fixed now that all the enemies were defeated.

The End

The Warriors

The year was 1986…A man was running from a fighter plane that was firing down at him. A missile exploded at his feet, sending him flying into a small pit. He hit his head on the way down, knocking him out.

His attacker was a mad scientist, who got him out. The man's hands were badly damaged. The mad scientist put him in a costume and added a microchip that helped the man recover quickly. Through experimentation, he was given power to control fire. He was named Flame Claw.

In 1989…A young man was playing laser tag. He got eliminated after getting hit by a laser, but then he stumbled and fell off a tower in the corner, into the darkness.

Minutes later, a troubled teen helps revive the young man and says, "You could have been there for weeks!"

They form a quick friendship. But the troubled teen was a very bad influence. They started robbing banks. A policeman stopped them from committing another robbery. The two ran, but the new friend was hit in the back by the policeman's gunfire.

The young man ran outside and got electrocuted at a nearby power station. Before the police could come, the mad scientist found him and took him to his lab.

Through the experiments, the young man learned that he gained the power to fly. The scientist created a suit, including a small staff with a blade on the end. He was named Slasher.

Now it is 1999. Over the years, the scientist has experimented on Flame Claw and Slasher. The two have harbored no ill will against the scientist, who, in his own twisted way, wants his two experiment subjects to stop crime, now they are known as the Warriors.

So, they are sent on a mission. They enter a secret villain lair. An armored guard finds them.

"Who are you?" he demands.

"None of your business," yells Flame Claw as he fires his blaster at the guard, killing him.

Three figures approach: A green blob, an armored soldier, and a man dressed in black.

The blob grows and decides he is hungry. He swallows Flame Claw and Slasher whole. The giant blob sits down and burps.

Inside the blob, a zombie is hungry. It creeps toward the duo. Flame Claw fires from his blaster, destroying the arcane creature.

The two then blast their way out of the blob.

The man in black does a jump kick at Slasher but misses. Slasher stabs through the man's chest, killing him.

"Me? Now?" says the armored soldier, now frightened that he is outnumbered.

"Now," says Flame Claw as he blasts him.

Alarms and lights fill the air as a camera views Flame Claw. Flame Claw destroys the camera with a blast from his gun.

An armored robot approaches.

"DESTROY!" it says as it fires a blaster.

Flame Claw's gun is shot from his hand. Flame Claw unleashes his claws and stabs through the robot, destroying it.

The Warriors then find the main power for the lair. An armored guard emerges from the shadows. Flame Claw fires a blast, but it bounces off its chest.

The guard fires something that envelopes Flame Claw in some thick goo, trapping him.

Slasher fires a blast from his staff but misses the robot. The robot then armors up and announces: "You must fight leader! Here he is!"

The leader rises from the floor. It is a huge armored robot.

"So...we have visitors, Matrix? They should know that I am a shape changer! Eat this, newcomers!" the leader says as he fires a blast from his chest.

But Slasher deflects the blast with a blast of his own.

Leader changes into a man, muscular with a necklace and shades.

"You're nothing but a loser!" says Leader as he fires a blast, missing Slasher.

Slasher fires back, hitting Leader in the face.

"Had enough shape changer?" Slasher says.

Leader transforms again, this time as a man in black, including a black cape and hat.

"I come in a gesture of friendship. Trust me!" Leader says while holding out his hand.

But then Leader fires a blast from his hand. Slasher blocks it with a force field. Leader transforms into a werewolf, extending sharp claws and a blade out of his hand. Slasher knocks the blade out of Leader's hand, then rips off his clawed glove. Leader growls with fury.

Slasher kicks Leader across the face. Leader claws Slasher across the chest with his other clawed hand. Slasher stabs through Leader's throat with his bladed staff.

Leader reverts to his natural form. He is now an old man.

"Growing…ol…old! Out…out of…con…cont…control…" Leader gurgles as he falls forward onto his face.

Slasher hears something from behind, so he turns to see a warrior in fencing gear.

"Die human!" the fencer screams with fury as he swings his sword.

Slasher blocks it with his staff, then slashes across the fencer's chest. Then Slasher wildly slashes some more, hacking away at his enemy. Finishing off his enemy, Slasher is panting as he stumbles toward Flame Claw.

Slasher then uses his power to release Flame Claw from his slimy and gooey prison.

The Warriors then leave the lair after setting up explosives. The lair is destroyed in a massive explosion.

The Warriors are then ambushed by space pirates, who damage their uniforms and take away their weapons. But they fly off, in search of other adventures.

They see large ship, which sucks them in.

"Not one of these!" groans Slasher.

A cloaked man with black and white streaked long hair and sunglasses stands before them, holding a blaster.

"Who are you?" he asks.

"We are mutants. My name is Flame Claw, and this is Slasher," says Flame Claw.

"We have hijacked this ship. We are trying to defeat the Space Warriors," says the man as he pulls down his shades, having a gleam in his eye.

"We'll help you," says Flame Claw enthusiastically.

Suddenly, a blast shoots through the man's chest.

"We'll avenge you! We'll stop them!" growls Flame Claw with determination.

The ship has been boarded by Space Warriors.

A muscular, heavily armed man with long hair and a scar down his face screams for his men to attack.

"No way, pal!" says Flame Claw as he slashes across a Space Warrior's chest.

Another Space Warrior fires at Slasher, who blocks the shot with his power, then punches the Space Warrior in the face.

More enemies arrive, but a few others join the Warriors: A cloaked, masked man and a muscled man with blades. They take out five Space Warriors.

"Most of my men failed. But I won't!" yells a muscular man holding a ball and chain as he is flanked by three more men.

One of the three fires his blaster, which hits the cloaked man in the chest. He cries out in pain as he dies.

With a rush of energy, the muscled man slashes across the sides of two of the men, then decapitates a third. He then hurls a curved blade which goes through one of the first two men, then digs into the other.

The leader swings his ball & chain, which slams into Slasher's ribs, a crunching sound filling the air. Slasher quickly heals himself.

Flame Claw slashes across the leader's chest. A blast from Slasher grazes the leader and the blade man slashes him with a blade. The leader punches flame claw. The blade man hits the leader with a blast from his necklace, killing him.

Having rid themselves of the attacking Space Warriors, the ship continues. As they travel, they can make repairs to the ship. In space, they approach an asteroid belt.

Asteroids pummel the ship, forcing it to crash land into a nearby planet.

Only the Warriors, along with their bladed friend, survive.

Suddenly, right after they get out of their ship, three massive beings emerge from the nearby ground.

"Attack!" one screams. The three jump into action. Slasher blasts one, Flame Claw torches another. But the third being picks up the blade man and squishes him in its hand.

A muscular, glowing man causes Slasher and Flame Claw to levitate, then he throws them several feet. Three guards then approach.

"Come with us!" one says.

A small ship picks them up while a larger ship looms overhead. Just as it lands inside the larger ship, the Warriors overpower the others in the ship and leave the small ship.

A muscular man with claws and with a mask in half black and half white stands before them. Seeing that they have overpowered his men, the man lunges toward them, clawing Slasher on the chest, then punching him in the face.

Flame Claw slashes back, slashing across the enemy's chest. The enemy slashes back. But Flame Claw slashes back twice, finishing off that enemy.

Flame Claw puts on the mask.

"High Contrast! Come to the main room!" booms over the speakers.

"That must be our clawed friend," says Flame Claw as they head to the main room.

Flame Claw kicks the door down.

A man is levitating before them, along with three spheres.

"I told you to take a pill," he says, mistaking Flame Claw for one of his men.

"Eat this!" roars Flame Claw as he claws toward the levitating man.

"Calm down!" the man chants as he causes Flame Claw to be pacified.

Distracted, he does not see Slasher as he kicks him across the face. Losing his concentration, he hits the floor in a heap just as the spheres smash to the floor, releasing a mist.

The man emerges from the mist, now a giant cyclops.

Entranced, Flame Claw now says, "Master!" as he claws Slasher across the chest.

Slasher bops Flame Claw on the top of his head. The cyclops yells as he lunges toward Slasher. Slasher punches him in midair. They collide. They quickly get up, then Slasher pounds the creature in the stomach, then kicks him across the face, knocking him down.

Slasher stomps on the creature's head, killing it.

Slasher helps Flame Claw get up.

A large, muscular, monster of a man smashes through the wall.

"Taste death!" he growls.

He claws through the air and knocks off Slasher's helmet, then backhands him. He fires a blast from his eyes, but Flame Claw deflects it with his claws.

The creature fires a blast from his hand, but Flame Claw dodges and claws into his head, killing him.

The duo escapes in a ship.

The End

The Scarabs-Part 1

The Scarabs are a group of four heroes. Starrush is very large and muscular. He uses his brute strength to stop enemies. Karate Master is a master of martial arts. Swordman is excellent with his sword. Blaster has excellent armor that allows him to fly. He carries blasters but can also shoot from the wrists of his suit.

They are engaged in a massive battle. A giant, muscular lizard man with claws assaults Starrush as it cackles in anticipation of its victory.

"C'mon!" Starrush roars.

ZAP! He blasts the lizard in the face.

"I can't see! I can't see!" it screeches.

"Dumb smart-mouth!" the big guy yells as he punches it in the face repeatedly.

It repeats that it couldn't see as the big guy punches him. Then with a final blast to the head, the creature drops with a crash.

The Scarabs cheer in victory. But then, an armored, winged soldier rockets through the air toward them. The soldier fires a missile toward them.

BOOM! The Scarabs barely dodge in time and are thrown in all directions.

"Ki-yi!" says Karate Master as he kicks the soldier, causing him to grunt.

Then, Karate Master throws two sais toward him at once. They dig into the soldier's shoulders. Karate Master tears off the soldier's mask and sees a bruised and bloody face underneath.

Then, Karate Master is blindsided by a set of nun chucks from an enemy ninja, causing spit to viciously erupt from Karate Master's mouth.

Swordman shoots down with his hip jets from above and slices into the shoulder of the ninja from up above and behind, causing the ninja to groan in pain.

CRACK! The ninja slams Swordman in the back. THWACK! The ninja then roundhouse kicks Swordman across the face. Swordman slices across the ninja's chest, then impales the ninja on his sword. Two large, armored, man-operated robot soldiers sneak upon the group from behind.

"Wimp!" says one as he slams Swordman, knocking him down.

"I'm getting hit more than a piñata," groans Swordman.

"Attack!" says one of the large soldiers.

Just then, Blaster blasts one of them in the helmet, causing it to break open.

"Raaa!" the soldier screams.

"Come with us. We're taking you in." says the other soldier.

"No!!" yells Blaster as he unleashes a barrage of laser blasts from his pistol.

The one with the broken helmet falls to the ground and the chest of the machine was blown open, exposing the small operator. The other robot soldier fires a laser blast from his helmet at Blaster, but he dodges it. The same soldier then swings his mace, causing the spikes to fly toward Blaster.

He blasts at the spikes, but they are explosive. Blaster is thrown to the ground. The explosion blows apart the robot suit of the soldier, revealing another small man. Blaster gets up, then the small man fires at him with his blaster and misses. Blaster blows him away with his blaster.

Meanwhile, Starrush is engaging in combat with a large, armored robot soldier.

WACK! They hit fists together as they both swing at the same time. Starrush blasts with his wrist blasters, causing a hole in the side of the armor to appear.

CRACK! Starrush punches the soldier in the face. KRONK! He punches down on its head. CRASH! He punches the head off. ZAP! He blasts off the legs. He then yells as he rips apart the torso. He staggers backward, panting from exertion.

Suddenly, another armored enemy uppercuts him. But then Karate Master kicks the enemy upward across the back, then he jumps back. Karate Master then throws two sais and a shuriken at the enemy as he turns. One sai enters the enemy's head, then the other Sai and shuriken hit the chest, killing the enemy.

Then a giant robot stomps the ground with its mighty foot, Karate Master dodging just in time. It roars in fury as it grabs Karate Master in its massive hand.

Starrush blasts it in the chest, causing the robot to laugh at the attempt. The eighty-foot robot then blasts at the heroes from its palm, but the heroes dodge in time.

Swordman jets up and slashes the fingers holding Karate Master. Starrush also jets up and punches the wrist and blasts it. Blaster blasts the robot in the head. It drops Karate Master.

Then the giant robot uses a combination of a tractor beam and suction to pull in the heroes. They slide down a shaft and into a room upon entering. Surprisingly, there is a lone ninja to greet them inside. With two swift slashes, Swordman takes him out.

Minutes later, they peek around a corner and see a guard. Starrush jets toward him and slams both fists into the guard.

"All clear!" says Starrush. "He must have been guarding something important."

He then smashes through the nearby door. Two armored guards are standing near a glowing sphere on a pedestal. One guard fires at Starrush and misses. Starrush blasts them both in the head.

Four ninjas quickly run up.

"Freeze!" the leader yells.

Starrush smashes two of them together by their heads. He then punches all the way through another guard in the chest, then throws him into the other.

Then a large, demon-masked enemy creeps up and starts blasting from his wrist blasters, laughing maniacally.

Swordman dodges and flies toward him with his sword, but then gets blasted in the chest. Starrush blasts the enemy, then picks up Swordman in his arms.

Blaster touches the sphere. A spike lifts from the floor, impaling him as volts of electricity course through him. He yells in pain and dies.

Starrush sets Swordman down.

"Noooo!" yells Starrush as he blasts the sphere with his wrist blasters.

Lights start flashing and alarms fill the air.

"This place is gonna blow! Let's get out of here!" says Starrush.

Karate Master quickly grabs Blaster's jets and sword. The two remaining Scarabs blast through the head of the giant robot and jet away as quickly as they can.

KA-BOOM! A massive explosion rocks the area and sends pieces flying in every direction.

Starrush and Karate Master stop to compose themselves, tears streaming down their faces. They find more fighting nearby.

An enemy sneaks up on them and aims his blaster. He has a cape and sunglasses. A sword and sickle are on his chest. A ring glows with power on his hand. He laughs at them, then fires two blasts. The Scarabs dodge.

"I am Crossblade!" he yells defiantly.

Suddenly, a robot appears from behind.

"STOP!" it says in its robotic voice as it blasts the gun out of Crossblade's hand.

The enemy fries the robot with his power ring. Two winged men approach, ready to attack Crossblade, who then raises a hand to the air, fingers outstretched. Light shoots from his fingers as he laughs.

A minute later, three massive robots smash into the ground close by.

"DESTROY THEM!" one says.

The Scarabs and the two winged men fly into action. One winged man slams a robot in the head with his fist. The other slams the hand of another as it tries to grab him. The same robot grabs Karate Master. Starrush then jets and slams into the face of another robot, then blasts into its chest, causing a large hole in the robot. A robot then blasts one of the winged men in midair and he falls to the ground, smoke billowing, then crashes.

"NOW FOR YOU!" the robot says to the other winged man as it fires a blast from its palm, frying the side of the winged man.

The robot slams down, trying to hit the winged man, but misses and pounds the ground. The winged man slams into the robot's face. The robot punches the winged man, smashing him, its fist the size of the man.

A tank-like robot fires at them and they dodge the blast.

Bolting into action, Starrush yells, "I'VE HAD IT!" and blows the tank up with a strong blast.

Karate Master and Starrush regroup. A robot fires and they dodge it, the blast going between them. Starrush fires a blast and Karate Master throws his sword at the robot. BOOM! It explodes.

Crossblade reappears.

"Now me!" he yells as he glows with power, light shooting out from his fingertips. He blasts Karate Master, killing him.

"Now I'm mad!" Starrush growls as he jets to the man and blasts him, causing the enemy to grunt as he dies.

A small explosion rocks the ground and sends Starrush flying. Three figures materialize out of the smoke: a fly-like man with a pike (the Fly), an armored winged man (Flying Fist), and a cyborg that has the body of a snake and carries a sword and scepter (Iron Snake).

The Fly leaps toward Starrush, swinging his pike. Starrush jets and rips through the fly man with his fists, tearing him in two. Flying Fist backhands Starrush, sending him flying.

Flying Fist extends blades out of his bracers and slashes across Starrush's chest. Starrush shoots a power rope from his bracers that tie up Flying Fist, but he breaks out with a yell. Flying Fist swings down and misses Starrush, hitting the ground. But the strength of the impact causes Starrush to stumble. Starrush then kicks Flying Fist in the groin, causing him to squeal in extreme pain.

Flying Fist composes himself quickly, then claws Starrush across the chest. Flying Fist flies up and extends claws on his boots and cackles as he soars down toward Starrush. But Starrush jets up and smashes him in the chest, then blasts him away.

Iron Snake approaches and fires three short but powerful blasts at Starrush with his scepter, none of the blasts getting a direct hit, but knocking Starrush around like a ragdoll. Iron Snake then swings his scepter and connects with Starrush's stomach, knocking the wind out of him. Starrush blasts the scepter, destroying it. Iron Snake forces himself onto Starrush, trying to attack with his sword. Starrush punches him in the face.

Iron Snake screams, "DIE!" as he electrocutes Starrush with his power.

Starrush backhands the serpent man with all his strength, smashing his face and killing him. Starrush leaves.

Minutes later, Iron Snake is found by others from his squad, including a changeling named Kang, that wears a purple costume with a yin & yang on it, a lion man (Lion Man), and a feral wolf-like man that has large claws named Wolf.

"I'll find the one who did this," grunts Kang as he transforms into a bat and flies away.

Kang finds Starrush. He transforms back into his human form and punches Starrush in the face. The other two had followed, so Wolf growls and leaps for Starrush, missing him. Starrush punches him in the head. Lion Man attacks, but Starrush punches him as well.

"C'mon!" Starrush howls, stepping into an intimidating fighting stance.

The changeling sneaks from behind and tries to grab Starrush, but Starrush sidesteps and trips Kang, causing him hit heads with Wolf, knocking both unconscious.

Lion Man claws Starrush across the face. Starrush punches him.

A wraith-like man in a cloak threateningly drifts up. Starrush blasts at him but misses.

The wraith stumbles back, then removes the hood. It's Blaster!

"Hi, friend, remember me?" says Blaster.

Just then, the lion man roars, and leaps toward him.

Blaster throws two daggers at lion man, killing him.

Starrush quickly puts the lion suit on.

"The spike was an illusion. A cloaked spider-like monster quickly took me seconds after you left the giant robot," Blaster explains. "It tried to kill me, but I killed it instead. I then took its cloak."

Kang and Wolf come to their senses. Blaster and Starrush convince them to join up with the rest of them. They decide to leave the battleground.

But three giant, armored, winged robots fly up and start to attack.

The men blast and fight. Blaster gets his cloaked ripped off, but eventually, the robots are destroyed. The men then find two ships and blast their way out of the battle.

They then get some time off to relax at the beach.

Part 2

Nuclear Man is a hero. One day, to protect the city, he was flying over it, looking to stop crime. A brick suddenly hit him in the face, then when he slowed, a power blast hit him. He saw Power Blob, an enemy blob-like creature down below. But then a ship was also heading toward him and started firing. He used his power to create a force field, then destroy the ship, causing it to explode. The blast partially hit him, which caused him to fall into the river below.

Minutes later, Nuclear Man has changed into punk clothing and is walking down the street when he sees Power Blob coming toward him. The green blob fires a blast but misses him.

"Stop!" he hears a yell from behind, "We'll help you!"

Four other heroes stand before him: Kang, Starrush, Blaster, and Wolf are there.

"I know you guys!" Nuclear Man says in excitement, but trips and falls as he stumbles after seeing the blob right behind him.

He quickly gets up, then punches the blob, who growls.

Starrush blasts the blob with his power, but the blob seems to like it as he starts to grow several stories high. The Air Force happened to be doing a maneuver nearby and an F16 pilot decided to attack the giant blob, firing missiles and its machine guns at the blob, which just absorbs the attacks. The blob then fires a blast from his eyes, destroying the plane.

Power Blob then fires a blast from his hands, trying to hit Nuclear Man, but Nuclear Man leaps out of the way. The blob then stomps, trying to crush and absorb Nuclear Man, but he dodges that as well.

Nuclear Man then fires a blast into the blob.

"Too much power!" Power Blob groans then explodes, slime flying in all directions.

With Nuclear Man's help, in addition to mystical arts and latest technology, the assembled heroes were able to bring Swordman and Karate Master back to life. The heroes assemble against a massive force that is trying to attack the city.

<u>Starrush-</u>Starrush sees a caped enemy dressed in black with a Union Jack on his chest.

"Wimp!" the villain harshly whispers, "I've seen you fight! You've got weaknesses!"

Starrush punches him hard in the face, sending him sprawling backward. The villain fires a blast, but Starrush dodges. Then the villain whips out a dagger and slashes Starrush across the face.

Starrush abruptly punches then kicks the villain, who struggles to get up. The villain then tries to stab again, so Starrush finishes him off with a blast from his fists.

<u>Blaster-</u>Meanwhile, Blaster is going to break into a massive tank that is heading toward the city. A bat-like creature descends in front of him. He blows it away. Blaster then finds an air vent on the

back of the tank. He enters. He then sees that someone is being held captive, a large machine looming above them. A guard is standing watch. Blaster fires a blast from his gun, which causes the machine to land on the guard. The captive is then able to break out.

Blaster enters the room.

The captive says, "Thank you! I am General Striker!"

Suddenly the guard pushes the machine into General Striker.

The guard then fires his gun, but Blaster dodges and roundhouse kicks him across the face. He then follows up with a punch to the face, then shoots him.

"Let's go!" says General Striker.

But then, an officer with an Uzi comes into the cell. Blaster and the officer fire at each other but miss. General Striker kicks the officer, knocking him out.

Suddenly, a werewolf attacks General Striker, ripping at him with his claws. But Blaster scares it off.

Swordman- Swordman faces off against a cloaked figure with a dagger. Their blades clash. The enemy slices across Swordman's thigh, causing him to fall.

"I will kill you!" the cloaked enemy screams in desperation as is going to bring his dagger down on Swordman.

But mustering his strength, Swordman kicks him into a wall, then hurls his sword which decapitates the enemy.

Another enemy emerges from the shadows. The enemy is in a bird suit. The birdman extends claws from his hands and feet and flies toward Swordman. Swordman slices across birdman's chest, punches him, then impales him on his sword.

BOOM! A cannon on a small tank fires but misses Swordman.

"STOP!" comes a booming voice from the tank.

Karate Master- "Stop!" shouts a soldier at Karate Master.

Karate Master swiftly takes out the soldier, then puts on the soldier's uniform. Karate Manager enters the humongous tank in the rear using an access card. But two guards figure out he is an enemy, so they try to stop him. He knocks them out then takes off. But an alarm starts blaring and three more guards appear in front of him, guns drawn.

Kang- "Stop!" an enemy soldier shouts at Kang from behind.

Kang then changes into a massive Rottweiler and rips the soldier apart as the unfortunate man screams in pain and terror. When finished, Kang changes back and pulls out his gun.

Another soldier approaches. Kang changes into a werewolf.

"FREEZE!" the soldier screams in desperation and fires his gun but misses.

Kang shoots him in the head, then slashes him across the throat and eats his flesh.

"Stop!" screams a caped cyborg.

Wolf-Wolf breaks into another part of the tank. He enters a large air vent. In one of the rooms, he sees three men working on a large weapon and a cloaked figure supervising the work. One of the men is working very slowly.

"Get back to work!" screams the cloaked figure.

"No! I'm not afraid of you!" screams back one of the workers.

The cloaked man fires a sharp pronged blade that pins the man against the wall while his screams of pain fill the air.

Another worker throws down his helmet, then kicks the cloaked figure. The worker then fires a blast from his tool into the cloaked man's face.

Wolf drops down from the vent above. The two remaining workers jump at the sight.

"Calm down! I'm on your team, turbo!" Wolf says.

He picks up a large machine gun and hoists it in the air saying, "Let's get the heck outta here!"

They leave the tank.

Nuclear Man-He uses his mind powers to speak to the rest of the group…Starrush, Blaster, Swordman (as he destroys the tank), Kang (as he shoots his enemy), Karate Master (as he finishes off the last soldier with his sword), and Wolf. They all regroup and defeat the enemy.

The END

Starforce & the Mystery of the Sphynx

Starforce includes the following heroes:
- Skinny-He is skinny.
- Muncher-He has quite the mouth, but he can back it up with his brute strength.
- Basher-He likes to break stuff.
- Question-He is mysterious.
- Cyclone-He can turn himself into a cyclone.
- Sight-He wears a visor over his eyes.
- Creature-A monster of a man.
- Sceraly-He is a fighter and a soldier.
- One-eye- He is a cyborg where half of his face robotic.

Sight sees on their systems that there is trouble after they have located a villain's hideout, inside a massive sphynx. The group splits into groups of three and decides to infiltrate it.

Skinny/Muncher/Basher-At the entrance, they see a statue of an Egyptian warrior. In a moment of carelessness, Basher puts his hand on the arm of the statue. It moves, then a door opens. The three enter. The heroes step inside a large computer room.

Unbeknownst to them, someone is watching through a one-way mirror high above on the wall. The man pushes a button. A bulky lizard with sharp teeth enters the room. Muncher slams into it, punches it in the head, then kicks it in the face.

In anger, the lizard fires a blast from its eyes at Muncher. The blast misses, but the explosion caused by its impact throws Muncher across the room. Muncher pulls out a gun and shoots the creature, killing it.

"I'll get them myself," whispers the watching figure to himself as he grabs his gun and puts on his helmet.

He then smashes through the glass and lands squarely on his feet on the floor below, landing behind the three heroes. He aims his gun at them.

Question/Cyclone/Sight-These three are at the face of the sphynx.

Cyclone senses something. He turns to see a costumed swordsman about to attack Sight. He fires a blast from his hand, taking out the attempted assassin.

The mouth of the sphynx opens. The three enter.

Meanwhile, inside, the evil leader sits on his throne, his men standing near as they watch their intruders through a large crystal ball. Prisoners are chained to a wall nearby.

They see the three heroes begin to enter a dark doorway. Cyclone senses trouble brewing.

The leader presses a button. It teleports two captives, who are changelings, into the same room as these three heroes. One changes into a werewolf and the other changes into a large cyclops with a mace for a hand.

Question barely dodges in time as the mace comes crashing down near his feet. Cyclone dodges the next smashing blow from the cyclops. Sight is slashed across the chest by the werewolf.

The two creatures are vaporized by blasts from Cyclone's visor.

Cyclone senses another presence as a small group of zombies and a swordsman are about to attack from behind.

<u>Creature/Sceraly/One-eye-</u>As they enter the building through the rear entrance, a big armored man with a cape stands menacingly before them. Creature lunges at the enemy as he swings his sword. He is knocked back by a blast from the enemy.

Sceraly fires a blast from his laser gun, but the enemy blocks it with a gesture from his hand.

Suddenly, a skateboarder with a skull mask and a mohawk hits a jump and flies over the enemy. Distracted, the enemy is hit in the back by another blast from Sceraly.

The skateboarder swings a spiked ball and chain, hitting the man in the chest and he goes down. The skateboarder joins the group of three heroes.

Suddenly, four other figures wearing skull masks emerge from the shadows and approach menacingly.

<u>Skinny/Muncher/Basher-</u>The figure drops in front of them, ready to fight.

"Get down!" Skinny yells to his buddies as he pulls out a heavy machine gun and fires away.

The hundreds of bullets smash all around the enemy with only a few hitting him, which only knock him back due to his armor.

Muncher then slashes across the enemy's chest with his sharp claws, punches him, then punches again, this time with all his might. His fist enters through the armor and into the enemy's chest. He slumps to the floor, bleeding from his chest.

The trio then sees three doors, so they split up again.

Skinny enters a room and sees a heavily armed enemy in front of him. He fires away, killing him. He puts on the uniform and grabs the weapons. Over a speaker in the room, it announces for all guards to go the main room.

He gets on a nearby scooter and follows the signs. As he arrives, he sees a heavily armed man wearing a skull mask as he is speaking to his four men. Skinny tosses a grenade. It blows the leader's legs off. His torso lands on the floor and the man lets out a few last breaths.

"Get him!" screams a guard with a beret as he fires at Skinny with his gun, who leaps over the blast.

Skinny then punches an armored guard in the face as he kicks another, also in the face. With his heavy machine gun, he blasts clean through another guard with a beret. He knees the other guard with the beret in the groin. He crumbles to the ground. The two armored guards and a creature aim their guns at Skinny.

Question/Cyclone/Sight-The zombies and swordsman laugh with glee as they get ready to fight.

Question punches the swordsman as a zombie grabs Cyclone. Question and Sight each blow a zombie away with blasts from their eyes as Cyclone fires a blast from his hands, taking out another. Question and Sight blow away the swordsman with simultaneous blasts.

One zombie is left. Cyclone uppercuts him, sending him careening backward and onto his head. He doesn't get up.

Three more figures appear.

"Stop!" howls a man on fire wielding a sword.

"Go no further!" yells an armored, bearded man, a bright glow surrounding his body.

"Yeah!" agrees an ugly man with a chainsaw.

Just as Sight is about to jump into action, the fire man summons fire demons. One swings at Sight, who catches his fist, then blasts with his eyes through his visor, killing the creature.

Two more demons approach. Sight takes them out too, but then the fire man binds Sight with chains of fire, then shoots fire at Sight, who only gets burned slightly.

Sight fires two rapid blasts, knocking the fire man back. The fire man then unsheathes his sword. Sight pulls out his sword also. To show his skills, he slashes across each side of the man's face as they fight. And then, he decides to finish the fight and hurls his sword through the fire man's chest.

Yards away, the bearded man is going up against Question. He hits Question in the chest with a blast from his hands. Question fires back. The man is vaporized.

Cyclone approaches the chainsaw man.

"Let me make this chainsaw a part of you!" the man screams maniacally as he swings it toward Cyclone.

Cyclone grabs it in midair and grunts with exertion as the maniac pushes with all his might. But Cyclone forces the blade back and cuts the man in half, blood spraying in all directions.

Gasping after their fight due to exertion, the trio then beholds a winged demon before them, its hands glowing with power.

Creature/Sceraly/One-eye-The three face off against the skull men. A skull man lunges with his sword and stabs Creature in the chest.

"Nooo!!" Sceraly screams as he pulls out a small machine pistol and blows two away, one of which had the sword.

"You'll pay!" One-Eye bellows as he blows away the others with his machine gun.

The two heroes see some creatures that are like horses. They jump on and ride. A blast hits the floor in front of Sceraly, causing the horse to rear back in fright, knocking Sceraly off.

A mohawked man in a cape laughs in triumph as his hands smoke from the power blast.

Suddenly, the creature stands up on two legs, then punches the guy with the mohawk, sending him sprawling backward and slamming into a wall. The creature then casts a spell that freezes the enemy. The other beasts also transform, one into a wizard and the other into a swordsman.

The mohawked man hurls off his costume, revealing a nerdy guy in a shirt and tie.

"Waste him, guys!" Sceraly shrieks.

Bullets fly as well as a missile. Seconds later, a bloody corpse lies on the ground, smoke billowing up from it through the air.

Skinny/Muncher/Basher-Skinny fires dozens of rounds into the remaining soldier with the beret. The two armored guards swing their maces and miss as Skinny leaps above them, then tosses a grenade down between the two. BOOM! Only bits remain.

Three soldiers appear, one of which is a beast.

In one of the other doors, Muncher finds a cloaked figure in black. The figure touches Muncher on the shoulder, causing him to pass out. A caped man appears and punches the cloaked figure, knocking his hood off, revealing a skull face.

The figure grabs the caped man.

"No…" the caped man says, then materializes.

"No!" Muncher says and pulls out his pistol. He then fires into the cloaked figure's chest, killing him.

Muncher dodges just in time as two ships heading toward him fired at his feet. Then, one of the ships teleports him inside their ship.

Muncher is now inside a laboratory.

"Hello," a man-tiger growls. "I am a grrr…scientist. I want to do some tests on you."

Muncher kicks him in the throat. As the man-tiger is gasping for air, Muncher hooks him up to an experimentation table. Muncher releases thousands of volts into the creature's head.

Muncher sees the door to the cockpit and quickly comes up with a devious plan. He grabs the man-tiger and hurls him through the glass door. Glass shatters in all directions. He picks up a small spear and hurls it through the pilots back as he is in the pilot's seat. He quickly sets a small bomb for five minutes amidst the chaos.

After releasing two prisoners, Muncher quickly gets into an escape pod with them and flies out, seconds before the ship explodes. But then his ship gets swallowed up by a larger ship that has the face of a tiger.

Elsewhere, Basher is outnumbered. A ghoul with a spear and sword, a ninja, and a masked archer stand before him, ready to kill.

The ghoul hurls his spear. Basher blasts it out of the air with his shotgun. Basher then punches the archer as he is readying an arrow. The archer slams into the ghoul. The ninja kicks Basher in the back of his head, causing him to be dizzy and fall to his knees.

As the ninja is about to decapitate Basher, a shield blocks the blow. It is a masked warrior dressed in black, with a sword and shield. The warrior slashes the ninja across the chest, then stabs through the ghoul.

The archer grabs Basher from behind. But Basher grabs the smaller man and hurls him over his head. The archer grunts as he lands head first. But the archer has sharp instincts. He quickly fires off an arrow at Basher but misses.

The warrior fires a fireball from his shield, scorching the archer. The warrior leaps for the ninja. But the ninja has something in his hand. The warrior sees that it is a spike bomb. A small weapon that shoots spikes in all directions.

"No! Don't!" the warrior screams and tries to block the attack with his shield.

The warrior and the ninja are filled with spikes.

"I…I…did it because of m…my honor," the ninja gasps as he dies.

"Leave me…" the warrior says to Basher.

Basher is alarmed to see a motorcycle speeding toward him, firing blasts from its guns. The masked man on the motorcycle says, "No one escapes us!" as he speeds toward Basher.

Question/Cyclone/Sight-The winged demon unleashes a wicked smile as he positions himself before them, ready to attack.

The demon fires a blast at Sight as he chants, "You will be strong, greedy, cruel, and a master of magic!"

Sight transforms into a similar winged creature. He roars with fury.

Just then, a trap door opens nearby.

"Get in! Quick!" a man yells from the hole.

Question and Cyclone quickly enter the trap door just as a large cross and some machine guns emerge from the floor.

"I'll get them!" the first demon screams as he flies away.

"Your friend isn't safe," the man says. "He is now a minion of Warlock," he continues.

Another man guards the stairs, gun ready. Another sits at a console.

Elsewhere, Warlock has transformed another man.

"You will be wicked, strong, mystical, and powerful!" Warlock chants as he uses his power on the man.

The man becomes a bull-like creature with sharp teeth. The bull-man laughs as he feels the power.

"Now, we will launch our big attack!" Warlock screams.

"Appear! Appear!" he chants as he summons a large hammer-wielding cyclops from the netherworld.

Minutes later, the demons find the spot where Question and Cyclone had escaped.

"There it is!" Warlock screams in victory.

The cyclops fires a blast from his hammer, which destroys the cross and guns. The four creatures enter the hole.

The man guarding the stairs fires his gun at the cyclops, hitting him in the chest. It has very little effect.

Cyclops and Question stand for a split second in amazement at the demons.

"Cyclone!" Cyclone yells as he changes into a human cyclone and destroys the cyclops.

The three demons begin their attack.

<u>Sceraly/One-eye-</u>Sceraly, One-Eye, the skateboarder, and the three transformed steeds see a ninja and a samurai.

"Hello," says the samurai pleasantly.

"Goodbye!" bellows the former steed that is now a wizard as he fires a blast from his hand.

But suddenly and quickly, a large dragon descends from above and blocks the blast with its fire.

"Do not attack us! We are friendly!" the dragon admonishes.

Our group of heroes say goodbye to their newfound friends and press forward. As the group presses on, they do not see a silent figure approach from behind. The stranger attacks the wizard who was at the end, hitting him with an electric shock, then sends him through a portal.

The others turn to see their new enemy.

"I am Killer Bee! I will get all of you!" says the man in yellow spandex with a leather jacket.

Killer Bee then fires a blast from his visor, blinding the original steed, who he uppercuts with his tremendous strength.

"He is very strong. Kill him…" the steed gasps as it dies.

The skateboarder hurls a large dagger, which lodges in Killer Bee's chest, killing him. The skateboarder then puts on Killer Bee's suit.

The swordsman steed changes back into a riding creature. Sceraly jumps onto its back. Shortly after, a man in a trench coat riding on a large bird flies down and blasts the beast with his 9 mm, causing it to scream in pain.

Skinny/Muncher/Basher-The motorcycle whizzes past Basher, barely missing him. As it passes, Basher fires a blast into the motorcycle.

The masked man gracefully flips in the air off the motorcycle as it explodes. The masked man then destroys Basher's shotgun with his nun chucks, punches Basher in the face, then shocks him with a powerful stun gun. He throws Basher into a pit.

Seconds later, when Basher gains consciousness, he finds a guard standing over him. Basher unleashes a flurry of punches. The guard doesn't get up. Basher takes his uniform and weapons, then gets out of the pit. Inside the giant cavern, a jet is flying toward him. He fires from his gun and shoots it down. The explosion throws him a few feet.

A giant robot then tries to stomp on him. He dodges, then gets inside the foot of the machine by blasting into it. An armored guard holding a mace stands before him as he gets out of the trap door that leads from the leg of the machine.

"Intruder!" the guard screams in alarm.

Question/Cyclone/Sight-The demons start firing blasts at Question and Cyclone.

"Question!" says Question, which transforms him into a large golem. He punches their former friend, then fires a blast which captures him. The punch and the blast transform Sight back into a human form.

The bull demon screeches in fury. Cyclone fires a powerful blast from his hands, hitting the creature.

"Thank you…" are the man's last words as he transforms back into a human, only to die.

Question and Cyclone get ready to defeat the lead demon.

"Impressive," he growls, a wicked grin creeping to his lips.

Question then locks grips with the creature. He fires a blast, hitting the creature's mystical necklace. The demon changes into a man with a cape and long hair.

"I'll be back!" he says as he quickly escapes.

The three are back together.

Sceraly/One-eye-Sceraly fires a blast from his laser blaster, hitting and killing the bird. The man falls, losing his disguise. As he is falling, the skater (now Killer Bee) blinds him temporarily with a blast from his visor, punches him, then uses super speed to run around him, which causes a small whirlwind, which lifts him up.

The man burns off his clothes with his power. He is now dressed in all black, a thunderbolt emblazoned on his chest.

"I am Thunderblade!" he roars as a taunt.

"Attack!" One-Eye says.

Sceraly roundhouse kicks Thunderblade across the face, then punches him. Thunderblade then hurls Sceraly away with his power.

Killer Bee speeds over to Thunderblade, punches him in the face, then kicks him in the chest. His next punch is caught in mid-air by Thunderblade, then Killer Bee receives a shock by Thunderblade. One-Eye punches Thunderblade in the face.

"Now?" Killer Bee asks One-Eye.

"Now," says One-Eye as all three unleash their attacks. Sceraly with his blaster, One-Eye from his hand blaster, and Killer Bee with a blast from his visor. The blasts tear Thunderblade apart.

Suddenly, a muscular, monstrous villain appears, along with a group of armored soldiers, then blasts Sceraly.

Skinny/Muncher/Basher-"Destroy!" the guard yells as he tries to choke Basher.

Meanwhile, Skinny stands before two armed guards and a creature. Skinny blows away the two armored guards. The creature knocks Skinny's machine gun away. Skinny punches the creature in the face.

Elsewhere, Muncher and his two newly freed friends cautiously and quickly get out of their escape pod.

"Be ready!" Muncher says shortly before hundreds of shots ring out in the air.

Several soldiers lay dead at their feet and the three are briefly disgusted by the carnage.

But then they are attacked from behind. One armored guard bashes one of the former prisoners in the face with its mace and another guard punches the other former prisoner so hard in the face that he dies.

"No!" Muncher yells.

Suddenly, a large alien creature grabs Muncher with one of its electrifying tentacles, shocking him.

Muncher pulls out a pistol and fires several rounds into the creature's head, killing it. Muncher then simultaneously punches and kicks the two armored guards. He then fires at the two guards with his pistol but misses. He fires again, but his shots are blocked by their maces. He fires yet again, but the bullets bounce off the guard's chests.

"Okay then…" Muncher says as he whips out a heavy machine gun and fires away, blowing the heads off the two guards.

Their bodies tumble to the floor. Making sure that no one else is left, Muncher finds the cockpit and smashes through the door. He kills the two pilots, then takes the controls. He is able to track Skinny and Basher, who he teleports into the ship.

They get past their initial confusion, then they decide to head back home.

Question/Cyclone/Sight-The three combine their powers, so they can teleport back home.

One-eye/Killer Bee-Killer Bee and One-Eye scream out in anguish as they lose their friend. One-Eye transforms into a monstrous form.

Killer Bee unleashes a flurry of punches into the face of the enemy. The enemy then evades, then commands his followers to attack.

Killer Bee and One-Eye jump into action, fighting the armored soldiers. Killer Bee gets in a low blow, causing the leader to fall to his knees in extreme pain.

"YOU!" he screams as he fires a blast at Killer Bee and misses.

Suddenly, a blast tears completely through an armored soldier.

The shooter is a robot police officer on a motorcycle, along with four soldiers on jetpacks. One of the other armored soldiers fire a blast, destroying the motorcycle and sending the robot flying. Those on jetpacks join the battle. As one is taken out, Killer Bee grabs a jetpack and blaster.

Killer Bee blasts one armored soldier in the face with his visor, then blasts another with his new blaster.

The armored soldier leader pulls out a sword and shield as he laughs in anticipation. Killer Bee and One-Eye fire blasts, hitting him. The leader flies up into the air. Killer Bee flies over and slams into the leader, then punches him. They blast each other with their power. Killer Bee falls, but One-Eye catches him.

One-Eye then armors up and fires at the leader, hitting him. The leader then falls to the ground with a mighty crash.

Out of nowhere, a large, muscular man with a bat smashes the ground, causing a small earthquake, which knocks Killer Bee and One-Eye down.

"Batter up!" he yells.

One-Eye fires at him but misses.

"Now I'm mad!" the man howls in anger as he flexes his muscles, causing his clothes to tear.

One-Eye flies toward him, but is knocked back by a mighty punch, knocking him back into Killer Bee.

"No!" yells a birdman as he fires a blast, hitting the batter in the back and knocking him into a nearby wall.

The birdman then claws at the man, but it is blocked by a punch. The man then hurls the birdman away.

The man then transforms into a dark, blob-like creature, glowing with energy. It rips the birdman apart with a growl.

It turns to attack Killer Bee and One-Eye.

One-Eye grows into a giant with Killer Bee standing on his shoulder. One-Eye unleashes laser blasts and missiles into the blob, then stomps on it. But the blob grows. One-Eye blasts it in the face through his eye. The blob groans, then evaporates.

One-Eye and Killer Bee find a ship and return home.

Epilogue-The Stingers-A new enemy

The robot policeman had joined back up with Starforce. We find him battling a demonic, cloaked villain, who is part of the Stingers. The robot fires his blaster, while the villain blasts energy from his hands. The robot gets a solid punch in, then fires an array of blasts at his enemy.

Elsewhere, we find the lead demon previously mentioned, battling with Cyclone, who is in a new suit. They punch and blast at each other. Others fight nearby as well. One-Eye is fighting a robed figure. The figure tries to punch him, but One-Eye grabs the fist, then fires a blast from his hand.

Meanwhile, Killer Bee takes out a giant robot monster.

The End

The Blasters-Part 1

It is the year 2361. Three men traveled through time: Robin Hood (now Golden Archer), Desmond Walsh (an astronaut from the year 1990, now Starblazer), and Dillon Rhodes (from 1988-A fanatic about flying, including a knowledge of birds, and he was a skilled hang glider, now known as Birdman). As the Blasters, they were summoned to fight for all that is good. Through psychic abilities of the powers that be, they were brought up to speed on the times. They were also given new weapons and technology.

They are teleported to attack some evil monsters. Upon arrival, they jump into action. Golden Archer uses various arrows, including explosive ones. Starblazer uses a blaster rifle and a hand blaster. Birdman is a master of telekinesis and has claws.

The body count rises. But Golden Archer is captured while he is separated from the others. However, they track him down.

"FREEZE!" an armored guard screams, pointing a blaster after they free him.

Birdman takes out the guard with his shoulder blasters.

Another guard appears right after and yells, "You're under arrest!"

Birdman extends his claws and rips into the guard's shoulders, then slashes into his chest.

The heroes then come upon a sacrificial ceremony amidst pits of flame. Golden Archer fires an arrow, hitting the officiating priest in the back. Golden Archer then gets near the altar. He punches one priest and slices another with his sword, sending both into the flames. The captive, who is muscular and bald, breaks free. Starblazer blows away another guard with his blaster.

Unfortunately, the captive is hit by a guard and falls into the flames.

Then a huge flame creature emerges from the flames below. Starblazer blasts away at it and Birdman does a mental attack, then slashes it with his claws, killing it.

The trio continues, finding a small group of enemy soldiers. Golden Archer springs into action, kicking one, then stabbing him. He then throws a small bomb, killing three. He throws a knife, killing another. He throws a type of bomb that shoots out blades in all directions, killing another.

An enemy appears in a large machine and fires its shoulder Gatling guns. Golden Archer dodges. Small explosions erupt all around from the bullets hitting the walls. Golden Archer fires an explosive arrow, destroying the machine.

An enormous creature crashes through the floor and is ready to attack.

Three strangers emerge from the smoke. One with a bow and arrow (named Zandar), one dressed like a ninja (White Ghost, the psychic ninja), and one with a mask and a gun (Greystarr).

"Need any help?" says Zandar.

"Sure!" shouts Birdman.

All six attack the large creature, firing their weapons. Seconds later, the creature has lost its hand and screeches in pain and anger.

White Ghost sends it to sleep with his powers. It crashes to the floor.

Then, another large machine comes. This version is even larger. Golden Archer fires an arrow. It bounces harmlessly off the armor.

"ATTACK!" Screams Starblazer as he fires his blasters.

Bullets, arrows, and bombs fly. A flurry of explosions erupts. White Ghost and Birdman use their telekinetic powers on the operator. The machine crashes to the floor and explodes, which causes a hole in the roof of the structure.

The heroes call in a helicopter from their team, which picks them up. But it was being followed by a soldier in a massive suit. They fire at each other. The helicopter goes down, but fortunately, everyone parachuted out before the helicopter crashed.

The soldier follows them and screams, "Die! Die!" as he fires at them.

Golden Archer hurls shuriken, damaging the soldier's suit. Then Starblazer fires a blast from his hand, destroying the suit.

"The Critical Trooper will destroy you!" he shouts.

He then quickly presses buttons on his chest, arms, helmet, knees and side.

"Ha! Come and get it!" he laughingly says, then fires a blast, hitting the pilot in the arm.

The pilot screams and groans in pain, then fires back, but Critical Trooper deflects it with his armor.

Greystarr hurls a grenade, which explodes and throws Critical Trooper several feet. Greystarr then fires blasts from his handguns, but Critical Trooper yawns as it bounces off his armor.

Golden Archer takes out a dagger and advances toward the enemy. Critical Trooper punches him, sending him flying. Critical Trooper is then hit in the chest with a blast, then hurled from an explosion from behind. Birdman slashes at his back with his claws, then slams him with a telekinetic blast.

White Ghost uses his powers to calm him down. Critical Trooper then flies upward, then blasts at Greystarr, but only grazes him. White Ghost hurls a Sai, which destroys Critical Trooper's jet pack, causing him to fall and land hard, causing a small explosion.

Critical Trooper shakily gets up and says, "You're dead!" to the group, with his armor destroyed.

He fires a blast from his shoulder, killing the pilot.

"Now for the rest of you!" he furiously screams.

But Starblazer blows him away with his guns.

Suddenly, a tiger ship arrives and starts firing at our heroes. Several tiger soldiers descend in parachutes, then engage in battle with the group.

White Ghost slices the throat of one, gurgling sounds coming from him during his last breaths. He then hits another with two shuriken. Starblazer gets punched by one of the soldiers.

Birdman runs through one with his claws. Greystarr blows one away.

Then, the ship teleports them inside. The team jumps into action when they see several tiger soldiers. Blades gleam in the light as well as blasts filling the air.

After taking care of business, they find a door that looks important. They fire into it with their guns, then knock it down. A grenade hits the floor.

They toss me a gift, thinks Golden Archer as he kicks it back into the room, causing an explosion.

They finish off a few others that survived the explosion in the room. Come to find out, it was a small armory. Zandar grabs the heavy weaponry. They then find a holding cell. They release the captive, then give him guns and a uniform.

The group takes over the ship, then gather the captives into the hangar. They then open the door and force them out.

Outside, there is much going on as other ships are attacking. Golden Archer (now with a jetpack), Starblazer, and Birdman decide to lead an attack after leaving the ship.

Starblazer smashes into a cockpit of one of the enemy ships, then breaks the pilot's neck. Just then, Golden Archer's jetpack is blown off him and he starts to fall, smoke billowing from him.

Starblazer quickly flies and grabs Golden Archer and takes him back to the ship, then heads back out, along with Birdman.

They see four winged monsters. Starblazer uses his guns and Birdman uses his telekinesis and his claws to attack and defeat their enemies.

The tiger ship receives a critical hit, so everyone evacuates.

A large missile blasts off, the target being a nearby city. As it is taking off, Zandar is in its path. He grabs onto it as he releases his parachute. Birdman is flying nearby.

"I've got to diffuse it, Birdman!" he says as he opens a panel on the missile.

He rips out a wire, causing some loud beeping.

"It's gonna blow!" the soldier screams.

BOOM!

"NO! I'm gonna kill them," Birdman screams after witnessing Zandar's death.

They regroup. Greystarr, Starblazer, Golden Archer, White Ghost, and Birdman are crouching in a trench, seeing a group of enemy soldiers coming toward them.

"Everyone ready?" Birdman asks.

Then they come out, blades gleaming and guns blazing.

A large tank comes into view.

"Destroy!" is heard from the tank, with White Ghost and Greystarr in its sights.

Meanwhile, up in the air, Birdman sees four enemy soldiers flying toward him. He uses his excellent flying and fighting skills. He destroys a jetpack on one. He uses his telekinesis to destroy another soldier. He runs through two more with his claws.

Down below, White Ghost and Greystarr take over the tank. The others get in the tank and man battle stations, allowing them to destroy the enemy. They make it back to their base.

Part 2

The five heroes are teleported to an enemy base and they stand in front of it, in awe.

"Hey guys! Want some fun?" White Ghost says as he runs toward the base.

Meanwhile, inside the base, the enemy sees through their surveillance that the heroes are approaching their base. A variety of men approach to stop them, some firing guns.

The heroes use their weapons and skills as they shoot, slice and fight hand to hand. Greystarr fires his 9 mm handguns, hitting one in the chest. Birdman also uses his psychic mind attacks.

White Ghost jumps into a group of enemies and begins to fight like a madman. He roundhouse kicks an enemy. He then decapitates another, then hurls a Sai, hitting an enemy in the chest. He kicks another as he slices across the chest of one with his sword.

The heroes cheer in victory after they have defeated their enemies. They then make it inside the base.

Secretly, in the shadows, there is a group of five enemies who stand ready to attack. A punk, a cloaked man with a chained wild dog-like creature, a heavily armed veteran soldier, a winged sports-themed man and another in a cloak.

They face off. Starblazer fires from his blaster, but it is blocked by a blast from one of the cloaked men. Starblazer punches the punk in the face, then blasts from his hand, taking out the punk.

The sportsman slams an explosive hockey puck with his stick, but Golden Archer jumps out of the way of the explosion. In mid-air, the archer fires an arrow, which envelopes the end of the hockey stick in goo. The sportsman jets toward Golden Archer and slams both fists into him, knocking him back.

Meanwhile, Birdman fires a psychic blast, taking out the creature. Birdman then flies over the cloaked man and claws across the man's shoulders. Birdman blasts from his eyes into the man's chest, rips into him with his claws, then finishes him off with a blast from his hands.

"I'm gonna smash you!" says one of the cloaked men to White Ghost as he tries to punch him.

The swing goes wide, and White Ghost hits him with a Chinese star near his armpit. The cloaked man fires a blast from his hand, but White Ghost blocks it with his psychic power. The cloaked man then whips into a whirlwind form. White Ghost hurls a Sai, hitting the man in the chest, causing him to change back into his normal form. He is impaled on White Ghost's sword as he falls.

Feet away, Greystarr faces off against the soldier. The gunman whips his pistols around in his hands, then fires, grazing the soldier in his sides.

The sportsman grabs the soldier while he flies over and flies away.

"We'll be back!" the soldier yells.

Part 3

As the battle was raging, an evil warlord had seen what was going on.

"I will summon my men, the Thrashers!" he says to himself as he has them attack the Blasters.

The Blasters see a group of armed men coming toward them, ready to attack. Golden Archer fires an explosive arrow, killing some of them. A man in a black mask and a mohawk fires a blast from his gun, which breaks Golden Archer's bow.

A large zombie starts running toward Golden Archer. Golden Archer hurls a dagger, which doesn't do much damage. He then hurls all his remaining arrows by hand as he growls in anger.

The zombie explodes. Golden Archer decides that he needs something more. He decides to use his mystical stone.

"Give me power!" says Golden Archer as he grasps it.

Suddenly, the stone pulsates with power and glows. Golden Archer transforms into a winged demon.

"I MUST DESTROY THE BLASTERS!" he growls, then says, "Eat this!" to Starblazer.

His power envelopes the space man. Starblazer fires two quick blasts from his hands, into Golden Archer's chest. The blasts torch the newly transformed demon.

Starblazer is summoned by the Razors and takes off to join them.

Part 4-The Razors vs. The Thrashers

The Razors, led by Starblazer, decide to practice their skills and abilities at their headquarters.

Roboman has heavy armor. He wields a mace and nun chucks. He is taking on a robot.

POW! He knocks the arm off, then punches it in the head, knocking the head off. He then jumps back and fires an explosive spike from his mace, which blows up the robot.

He sees an obstacle course and enters. Guns blaze. He chuckles as the bullets bounce off his armor. He steps over a tripwire. He dodges a laser blast, dives through a flaming hoop, then grabs the flag, finishing.

Woody is in tribal dress, which includes a sword, shield, and mask. His shield has mystical power.

He begins his practice. A robot shoots flame at him, which he blocks with his shield. He then decapitates the robot.

A robot wielding two swords appears. He hits it with ice from his shield, then cuts through it with his sword. He smashes through a hole with spikes using his shield in front of him. He jumps onto a skateboard, then grabs the flag, finishing his practice.

Cool Cat is next. He wears shades, a dark uniform, and has lethal claws.

A large robot approaches. He destroys it by cutting through with his claws. A small ship flies toward him. He destroys it with his claws. A ball with spikes speeds toward him, but he leaps over it. Grabs the flag.

Flying claws is a beast with claws that can fly.

A missile flies toward him, but he dodges it. A metal wall comes down, blocking his way. FWOOM! He burns through it with his claws and power. A glowing ball floats near him, causing him to be curious. It explodes, sending him flying into a wall.

"I'm MAD!" he growls ferociously.

Another glowing ball comes toward him. He claws it, destroying it before it can explode. Then he grabs the flag.

Starblazer gets ready. Suddenly lights flash and there is loud beeping. It is announced that he is not a beginner. He takes off using his jetpack. Three robots appear. He blasts their heads off. A small missile flies toward him, but he punches it. He destroys another with a blast from his hand.

The Razors hear word of a large flame creature and his henchman attacking the city. They arrive on the scene just as the creature grabs a bystander and bursts him into flames.

"Razors! Attack!" yells Starblazer as he blasts a henchman in the chest.

Starblazer hits the henchman with another blast as Woody hits him with a fireball from his shield.

"What? My guard? Nooo!" screams the creature as he summons flame demons.

The Razors make short work of the minions as they blast, slash and slam the enemies.

Then, they team up on the creature. It screams in pain as it is pummeled with blasts and slashes.

The creature unleashes a torrent of flame. Starblazer blocks flame with a force field. Flying Claws blocks with his claws. The flame bounces off Roboman's suit harmlessly. Woody blocks with his shield.

But Cool Cat gets a little burned. Woody cools him off with some ice from his shield.

The Razors attack again, slashing and blasting. The creature slams to the ground, shaking everything nearby. The Razors get back to their base.

Suddenly, a large ship belonging to the Thrashers smashes through the training room and slams into Starblazer. A cloaked figure emerges from the ship and casts a spell on Starblazer, causing him to be lightheaded and nauseous, then passes out. The mysterious figure grabs Starblazer and leaves.

Flying claws flies after the ship, but the flame from the blast of the ship pushes him away.

The Razors regroup.

"Master has been kidnapped!" Flying Claws states.

"Let's get him!" says Roboman.

The four of them take off and arrive at the headquarters of the Thrashers. A flying demon emerges near the base.

"Stop!" the demon screams.

All four unleash their weapons and power, killing the creature. They break in and see four doors in front of them.

"Split up!" Flying Claws demands with determination.

Flying Claws enters his door and sees a martial artist. The man bows then jumps into action, kicking Flying Claws and connecting with his arm, a cracking noise filling the air. Flying Claws punches him, sending him flying into a stack of boxes.

Next door, Woody comes across a warrior with a long Morningstar attached to a chain. He skates closer. The warrior swings his weapon, which grabs Woody's sword. Then Woody shoots a fireball from his shield, which knocks the weapon away. He then slams into the warrior, shield first.

Kicking through another door, Roboman finds a large man in armor and with four arms. He holds weapons in each arm. Roboman slams him in the head with his nun chucks, jump kicks him in the face, then hits him with his club.

Cool Cat claws through his door. An armored guard starts blasting, but Cool Cat dodges. They punch each other at the same time.

Elsewhere, Starblazer is held captive. The leader, Wraith, stands before him. Starblazer breaks out of the bindings. The leader then causes him to hallucinate. The leader then appears to be a cyclops.

Starblazer punches him, which causes the spell to wear off. Starblazer breaks out and the heroes regroup.

"Retreat!" screams Wizard, spittle flying in all directions. "I'll get you!"

The Thrashers abandon their base.

Part 5-The New Blasters vs the Crashers

The President of the United States meets with the Crashers.

"I need you to destroy the New Blasters," says the President.

The Crashers, consisting of Strongman, Preacher, Power Man, Wolfman, and Wizard agree to do it.

Minutes later, come to find out, it was not actually the President. It was the leader of the Thrashers, Wraith. He begins to quietly monologue as he changes out of his disguise.

"They beat me before, but they won't beat the Crashers! Ha! Ha! Ha! The Thrashers will also join in too! I'll make sure they're gone!" he whispers maniacally. "Men-attack the Blasters!" he says into his communicator to the Thrashers.

Later and elsewhere, the Crashers arrive at the headquarters of the New Blasters. Power Man causes Preacher, a muscular man, to grow even larger.

"The power of the Lord is with me!" Preacher proclaims as he starts to rip open the building made of reinforced steel as Strongman punches through it as he growls.

"C'mon, Blasters! Y'all are a buncha chickens!" says Preacher.

"All right!" says Cool Cat as he runs to meet the intruders, being excited for the fight.

"Glorify!" says Preacher as he fires his blaster at Cool Cat, who blocks it with his claws.

Cool Cat claws at Preacher, knocking his helmet off then clawing him across the face. Starblazer appears behind Cool Cat and fires a blast from his palm, which puts Preacher back to his original size.

Roboman runs out and delivers a jump kick to Strongman's chest, knocking him back.

Power Man fires a blast from his hand, but Starblazer blocks it with his armor.

Strongman fires a blast from his wrist blasters, but Roboman dodges, then punches him in the face, smashing his sunglasses and knocking him down.

Power Man fires another, more powerful blast. Starblazer collapses to the floor.

Wolfman faces off against Flying Claws. Flying Claws delivers a flying tackle.

Woody faces off against Wizard. Woody shoots flame as he hurls a short sword at the master of magic. All that remains is a charred corpse with a blade protruding from its chest.

Both teams are in remorse as they have a fallen comrade, Wizard from the Crashers and Starblazer from the New Blasters.

"Use all of your powers and magic to bring them back," says Woody enthusiastically.

They do so and a new figure forms. The man has a space suit and a cape.

"You may call me Star Wizard. Be friends. They are coming," he says as he seems to be in a trance.

Another part of the wall blasts open. Wraith appears, flanked by Space Warrior, Doubly, Kabal, and Argus.

"Now you will all meet your doom!" Wraith says as he cackles with glee.

Power Man faces off against Wraith. Power Man fires blasts from his hands and Wraith blocks the attack with a magical force field. They both unleash full power. There is an explosion which kills them both.

Wolfman and Flying Claws face off against Space Warrior. Space Warrior fires his blaster, killing Wolfman. Flying Claws flies and claws through Space Warrior.

Woody and Flying Claws face off against Argus. Argus tosses a bomb. It kills all three of them.

Doubly faces off against Star Wizard. Doubly fires his gun repeatedly as he throws a net over Star Wizard. Star Wizard dies.

Cool Cat faces off against Kabal. He claws into Kabal's chest, killing him.

Doubly hurls a knife, hitting and killing Strongman. Doubly then gets shot in the chest by Radical.

Only Radical, Cool Cat, and Roboman remain.

The End

Part 6-The Newest Blasters

The heroes now all have new uniforms. Cool Cat's suit has more sharp edges. Roboman is dressed in black. Radical has a mask and is heavily armed. Greystarr has a new mask and is more heavily armed. Birdman looks even more bird-like and his powers have increased. White Ghost is more heavily armed.

An evil villain group was formed called the Conquerors. Ripper, the demon, with his claws and spikes, also likes his sawed-off shotgun. The Destroyer and Crusher are very strong. Killer is a cloaked creature with telekinetic powers. Scorpion has a powerful sting with his tail. The Cobra is poisonous.

The Blasters have heard of the Conquerors.

"Slime-Man, Fireball, Nuclear Man, Spike, and the Avenger were killed by the Conquerors," announces Birdman grimly.

"Then that means that we must stop them!" says Roboman.

"They are at Terror Forest!" says Birdman.

White Ghost and Birdman fly, while the others fly in their ship. They land.

"Who challenges us?" Ripper growls.

The two groups square off.

Ripper against White Ghost…

"Die!" screams Ripper as he fires his sawed-off shotgun.

White Ghost blocks the pellets with a combination of his telekinesis and slicing his Sai, causing them to shoot back at Ripper, who cries out in pain. White Ghost then puts up a force field with his power. Ripper tries to touch White Ghost, but the shield reflects the decaying touch and kills Ripper.

Destroyer leaps in front of Birdman. Birdman slashes across the giant's face. Destroyer punches Birdman in the gut, who falls from the impact. Birdman fires a telekinetic blast, which throws Destroyer hundreds of feet, slamming him into dozens of trees and killing him.

Roboman swings his mace at Crusher and misses. Crusher punches Roboman, killing him with one punch.

Scorpion rushes toward Greystarr. Greystarr hurls a grenade. Scorpion knocks it back with his tail. It explodes halfway between them, killing both.

The Cobra and Cool Cat face off. Cobra releases poisonous gas and wraps his tail around Cool Cat. Realizing he is about to die, Cool Cat gives it all he has, plunging his claws into his enemy's chest. Both die.

Killer faces Radical. Simultaneously, they attack each other. Killer with a psychic blast and Radical with his heavy machine gun. They mortally wound each other. With his last breath, Killer summons the powers of the Conquerors and gives them to Crusher, who is the only other one left.

The remaining Blasters, Birdman and White Ghost, stand in awe as their new enemy increases in power.

"Die!" growls Crusher as he fires a blast from his newly formed tail at Birdman, who dodges. White Ghost slices off the tail.

Then White Ghost and Crusher clash with their psychic powers. The ninja then stabs the villain in the heart. White Ghost and Birdman go back to their headquarters and try to regroup.

The End

Unbelievable Titan-Featuring: Standard Issue

A huge android looms over an unconscious hero. It is Frost Man.

CRUNCH! The android is obliterated with one punch by Scott Ryker, also known as the Titan. But many call him the Unbelievable Titan because of his great strength.

"Who are you?" Titan growls at the hero as he started to awake.

"Frost Man of Standard Issue! We're a group that takes out villains." Frost Man says.

"Oh yeah?" Titan says.

ZAP! Frost Man changes into his frost form, covered in ice.

"Now do you believe me?" he says.

"Not quite yet," says Titan.

Frost Man freezes a bird as it is flying by to give further evidence.

But then suddenly, a sleeping gas bomb goes off at Titan's feet, knocking him out and changing him into his human form.

A uniformed guard grabs Frost Man by the shoulder as he is checking on Titan.

"Hey, cube head!" the guard says as he points his gun at Frost Man and fires.

Frost Man dodges, then fires sharp icicles into the guard's chest, knocking him back. Frost Man then encases the man in ice.

Frost Man goes to get help. He travels by ice to get his friends: Telekinetic girl and Laser Blast.

"I found a large guy by the name of Titan, who got knocked out. I took out the guard, but then I left," says Frost Man.

"What?" Telekinetic Girl says.

"No!" Laser Blast says, "Let's get him!"

The trio arrives.

"Why did you leave me?" Titan yells.

"I panicked!" says Frost Man as he takes off.

"Come back!" Titan yells as he charges after him.

A huge boulder slams into the ground near them.

"Hey! Freeze!" yells a large costumed figure who is joined by an armed soldier.

"I'll take care of..." Titan says, but then gets slammed by the man, who sends him flying.

Standard Issue jumps into action, all three attacking the stranger with their powers: Frost Man with ice, Telekinetic Girl with her mind powers, and Laser Blast who is firing blasts from his hands.

After several attacks, they finally knock the man out.

The armored soldier starts firing his assault rifle, but Frost man blocks it with a thick wall of ice.

Laser Blast fires a massive blast and takes out the soldier.

Titan is thrown forward from a punch to the back.

"You shouldn't have done that!" Titan shouts.

With all his might, Titan slams his enemy in the face, silencing him forever.

Calming down, he changes back into his human form, Scott Ryker, with his clothing torn.

At his weakest point, an armored being blasts him with power, knocking him unconscious. Before Standard Issue can respond, the stranger picks up Scott and flies away using his jet pack. Standard Issue follows suit.

Minutes later, Scott is in a suit filled with gas that keeps him in human form. He is being transported in a flying ship. A cloaked man with a mohawk looms before him as Scott coughs.

"Kill him," the man growls menacingly to a ferocious blob-like creature.

"No!" Scott yells as he delivers a jump kick to the creature's face.

The creature latches onto him. He rips off the facemask and his fury transforms him into Titan.

"I'm gettin' outta here!" says Titan as he starts smashing the wall of the ship.

Outside, Standard issue happened to be attacking in the same place.

Titan leaps out of the ship and Telekinetic girl catches him with her power. They make it to safety before the ship crashes and explodes.

The End

VERSUS
East vs. West

In the country of Darok, the east and west thought differently. On one hand, the West wanted to control the world. The people in the East wanted total freedom. A war broke out.

The westerners were trained only lightly in the military. The West had white uniforms and had a skull as their symbol.

In the East, everyone wanted to govern themselves, so there was anarchy. People would kill each other for small reasons. The East had black uniforms. Their symbol was two eyes without pupils. They were destined to be destroyed, especially because the West had a cyborg that was highly skilled in battle. The soldiers in the East were having a hard time staying alive as they were getting slaughtered.

But one thing kept the East together and kept them as a threat to the West. It was an enormous A-bomb being carried by one of their bombers.

A very courageous soldier from the West used a jet pack and caught up to the bomber but damaged his jetpack in the process. He was in process of dismantling it when the East bomber dropped the bomb. The soldier fell through the air, grasping the bomb. The bomb slammed into the ground amidst the battle, causing minimal damage, but killing the soldier in the process.

THE END

Sergeant Wrath vs Red Devil

A fierce battle is in progress. Explosions and gun blasts fill the air. Sergeant Wrath and his men are in their ships and are attacking a giant machine. The machine is operated by Red Devil, an evil villain. The machine is in the same form as Red Devil himself, which includes a spiked mask and a red suit.

The fighting is fierce. Finally, after losing several ships, the Sergeants men finally destroy most of the machine. The head detaches, carrying Red Devil, who is trying to get away.

But an ambitious soldier leaps from his ship onto the ship of Red Devil's.

"No!" screams Sergeant Wrath as he knows that the courageous soldier is outmatched.

Red Devil slams the young man in the face, causing him to fall from the ship and to fall to his death.

The sergeant unleashes a flurry of blasts into the escape ship, causing it to crash. He follows the ship and lands nearby the crash site. The sergeant engages in battle with Red Devil. They punch and kick each other.

Sergeant Wrath fires a blast from his gun into the shoulder of Red Devil. He then hurls two grenades at his enemy. The first throws the villain away several feet, but the second turns him to bits.

The End

Freedom Fighter vs Killer Alien

An alien arrives on earth. He is on the cliffs near the ocean outside of Los Angeles.

"Must find a host!" it says.

"Stop!" yells a police officer as he is running toward it, his gun ready.

The alien fires a blast from his hand, shooting right through the police officer, killing him. The leader then takes on the officer's form, appearing somewhat like a police officer but a little like an alien monster.

Two officers approach.

"Get him!" one says.

The alien fires a blast, knocking them off the edge of a hill. One officer happened to have a small grappling hook, so they stop themselves from falling.

"Freedom Fighter! We need help!" calls one into his radio.

Minutes later, Freedom Fighter arrives. He has the latest technology and he defends the city by helping the police.

"Stop!" he yells commandingly at the alien, then fires his blaster, hitting the alien in the chest. The alien fires back, vaporizing Freedom Fighter's helmet.

"You dare do that?!?" Freedom Fighter screams.

He fires back, hitting the alien in the chest again. It transforms into a large, muscular cyclops. It punches Freedom Fighter, knocking his head back and causing saliva to fly from his mouth.

"I can shape change!" the alien says as he picks up Freedom Fighter by his uniform, then punches him, sending him flying.

Freedom Fighter hits the ground, then quickly gets back up. He fires and hits the alien in the chest. The alien transforms again, turning into a floating eye with an energy body. Freedom Fighter hits the alien in the eye with his blaster. It changes again, gaining armor. They fire at each other, but the blasts hit each other, cancelling themselves out.

Two figures step out of the shadows.

"STOP!" yells one of the figures in a booming voice, a shrouded figure with a glowing staff.

An armored soldier with a blaster is by his side. The alien forms a gun in his hand, but the two newcomers blast him.

The alien transforms into a large hulking creature and dives into the nearby ocean.

The two strangers take Freedom Fighter to their jet which changes into a submarine. While in the ocean, they get Freedom Fighter to a table.

"Get on there, boy. I am Super Ninja, and this is Armour" Says the shrouded figure. "We'll help you to be able to shape-change!" he continues.

They operate on Freedom Fighter. It is painful, and he screams. While Freedom Fighter is resting, the two others leave the ship and decide to stop the alien.

They find the alien underwater. They fire at each other. The alien punches Super Ninja.

"Let's go, dear brother!" says Super Ninja to the other.

"Wimps!" the alien whispers.

They escape without being followed.

"We fought the alien. We are wounded. He beat us!" says Super Ninja.

"Let's get him!" says Freedom Fighter as he transforms into an armored being that can breathe underwater. He enters the water, blaster in hand.

Meanwhile, a large sea creature appears before the alien with an armored swordsman on its back.

The alien slams the creature with his fist then blasts it.

"Why?" screams the swordsman as he grips his sword. "Say your prayers!"

"Oh yeah?" asks the alien as it punches clean through the swordsman.

The alien changes into a caped, muscular man with sunglasses on as he leaves the water and steps onto the beach.

The three track down the alien.

"I'll go!" says Super Ninja, gripping his nun chucks.

POW! The alien blasts through the ninja. Super Ninja falls, groaning.

"Wimp! I'll finish you off!" growls the alien as he moves toward the ninja.

Super Ninja whacks the alien with his nun chucks. The alien stomps on Super Ninja's chest, finishing him off.

"Nooo!" yells Armour as he swings his sword at the alien.

But the alien grabs the sword mid-swing and stabs Armour through the heart.

"Hey punk!" says Freedom Fighter as he taps the alien on the shoulder.

Then he uppercuts the alien, sending him sprawling backward.

The alien changes into a knight and Freedom Fighter changes into a warrior with a lance, cape and helmet.

They both transform into 80's rockers. Freedom Fighter clobbers the alien, who then leaves the human's body. Freedom Fighter changes into a space police uniform. He is now able to better defend the world due to his powers.

The End

Fighting Kid & Mr. Rock N Roll vs the Agents

The Fighting Kid is an excellent fighter in various martial arts. Mr. Rock N Roll has a special guitar that shoots notes that can catch his enemies. A group of oppressive agents are trying to stop them. The agents had killed the families of Fighting Kid and Mr. Rock N Roll.

Fighting Kid and Mr. Rock N Roll were walking downtown, when a secret agent said, "You're under arrest!" and pointed his gun at them.

Fighting Kid knocks him out quickly with a jump kick to the face. The duo ties him up, then Fighting Kid gets into the agent's uniform, then they tie him up. They then put the unconscious agent out of sight.

Fighting Kid calls into the station and says, "I've busted Mr. Rock N Roll."

Another agent says, "I'm on my way."

Minutes later, with a screech from his car, the other agent arrives. Fighting Kid is standing by Mr. Rock N Roll, pretending that he is taking him into custody.

"I'll take him," says the agent enthusiastically.

"No, you won't!" says Fighting Kid as he blows away the agent.

The two take off in the car and decide to attack the head office of the agency. They smash into the glass doors of the building, showering glass in all directions.

A group of agents emerge, guns drawn.

"Halt! Stop!" one screams in desperation.

Fighting Kid fires into the group with the car's weapons.

Mr. Rock N Roll sees a rocket launcher being pulled out. They quickly get out of the car. Karate Kid blows away an agent and Mr. Rock N Roll catches another with his rock music. Mr. RNR picks up the rocket launcher.

"You're under arrest!" comes from a large machine operated by an agent.

"Oh yeah?" says Mr. RNR as he launches a missile, destroying the machine.

Another group of five agents arrive, including another master of martial arts. Excited about the opportunity of matching skills, Fighting Kid squares off with the other fighter, then jump kicks, connecting with his face.

The duo leaves the building. A helicopter hovers overhead. The two shoot it down with their weapons. Fighting kid takes out three of the agents with his shuriken.

An agent flies overhead in a jetpack. Mr. RNR uses his music, capturing the agent. Unable to fly, the agent slams into the ground. They have stopped the agency.

The END

Firestones vs. Icecaps with Salem in the middle!

There were several independent situations where the Firestones and Icecaps were in conflict.

A space knight was soaring through the air riding his astro-horse. He was enjoying peaceful times when suddenly, he collided with a knight who was flying.

"You blew up my astro-horse!" said the first, in anger.

The other fired blasts from his hands but were blocked by the other's sword.

"You shall die…" said the rider.

Elsewhere, a man was walking down the street. Another man was walking by and was speaking an alien language.

"What?" said the first.

"Help me!" said the second as he punches the first in the face.

He then groans and is ripped apart by two reptilian aliens that emerge from his now bloody and torn body.

With a burst of light, the other man transforms into his hero form.

Elsewhere, a hero was flying and enjoying it when accidentally, he bumped into a flying demon, who then screams, "You shouldn't have done that," as he punches the hero.

The hero fires a blast into the demon's chest.

Elsewhere, a man was walking down the street, when suddenly, an armed man kicked him in the face while punching a nearby police officer.

The man punches the armed man in the face, causing spit to erupt from his mouth. The armed man then simultaneously punches and kicks the man. The man transformed into his hero form.

"What? How dare you attack Achilles!" bellows the man as he drew his sword.

"Oh no!" whispers the armed man in fear.

Elsewhere, an armored demon-like man was running down a city street when he bumped into a hero.

"How dare you!" yells the man as he grabs at the demon.

They lock hands and the air around them glows with energy as they use their powers.

Elsewhere, a hero was walking down the street when he saw a man punch another. Little did he know; it was a mugger that was being punched.

But with hostility, he approaches the man, who then glows with power.

The hero punches the other man, perceiving that it was an unprovoked attack. The glowing man fires a blast from his hands, hitting the hero.

Elsewhere, two heroes dressed in masks and dark colors are patrolling the streets while wielding their weapons. They see something in a dark alley and approach cautiously. Two robed figures emerged out of the darkness.

"You are not invited!" one growled.

The heroes jump into action and attack.

Elsewhere, a hero bumps into a man in a fedora and a trench coat.

"Who are you?" says the hero.

The mysterious man whips off his hat and trench coat to reveal a sword and shield.

The man slams his shield into the hero.

Elsewhere, two armored heroes wielding guns see a man who appears to be up to no good. The man howls with laughter. One of the heroes fires a blast, grazing the side of the man.

Elsewhere, there is yet another duo that bumped into each other. This time it was a werewolf and a hatchet-wielding hero.

"I'll kill you!" growled the werewolf.

"Wanna bet?" said the hero as he readied his weapons.

Elsewhere, a pilot is flying in his ship and testing out his weapons. He accidentally takes out another ship. The other pilot ejects and is about to attack as he flies over using his jetpack.

"I shouldn't have done that!" says the first pilot, with regret.

As this all happened, Salem is able to use his telekinetic powers to speak to all of them and say: "Stop! We are all heroes!"

They all decided to get along.

The End

<u>Mr. Destructo vs. Super Ant</u>
Christian Scott, a former archeologist, also known as Super Ant, is watching the news. He sees a crazed villain, Mr. Destructo,

saying that he wants to destroy everyone as saliva sprays from his mouth.

"I'll get him!" Super Ant whispers to himself.

Minutes later, he is taking off in his car to find the villain. As he is driving, he remembers how he acquired his superpowers.

Two years ago, he was leading an archeological dig in India. A giant ant came. It scared everyone else off, but Christian did not run. The ant was able to speak.

"Come with me," it said.

Christian followed the ant into some large, nearby caves. The cave network was a labyrinth. They came upon a stash of gems, along with some nectar that was flowing from the ground.

"Drink!" said the ant.

Although hesitant, Christian tried it and it was delicious.

The ant was very pleased.

"Now you can grow large like me or as small as regular ants," said the ant.

Christian felt very strange.

"Can I have some gems?" Christian asked.

"Certainly, at least a few," said the ant.

"Can you get me home?" said Christian.

He was teleported back home and was able to sell his gems to a collector.

Super Ant now breaks out of his reminiscing as Mr. Destructo comes into view. Super Ant slams into the villain with his car. Super Ant gets out of the mangled car.

"Stop!" yells Super Ant as he punches Mr. Destructo.

Mr. Destructo kicks Super Ant across the face, then throws him up against a wall.

Super Ant shrinks down.

"Huh? Where'd he go?" says Mr. Destructo.

Super Ant gets under his foot and causes Mr. Destructo to stumble. Mr. Destructo then tries to blast Super Ant from his eyes but misses. Mr. Destructo punches his small enemy, sending him flying.

But Super Ant, still small, smashes Mr. Destructo across the face, then blasts him in the chest. He kicks Mr. Destructo across the face.

Super Ant grows, then dwarfs Mr. Destructo.

"Give up!" growls Super Ant menacingly.

So, Mr. Destructo gives up and Super Ant turns him over to the police.

The End

The V-Men Battle Royale
Part 1-Origin of Black Knight

One day, an ex-con with a long rap sheet had just been released from jail. His name was Emrick Austin. He was driving down the street in a convertible, enjoying the scenery and considering his plans for his next scheme. At a side street downtown, a man in a cloak, carrying a glowing gem necklace stumbled into the street in front of him.

"Stop…please!" the cloaked man weakly called out.

Emrick pulled his car to the side of the street and got out.

"Take this…it will give you enormous powers," he croaked out with effort.

Emrick took it and drove off quickly. He heard in the distance, "There he is! Get him!" as he saw the cloaked man being shot in the street behind him.

Emrick got home to his ramshackle apartment. He put the necklace on. His clothes transformed into spiked armor with a hood and a cloak. He also had claws, a mace and a small sickle attached to a chain.

He became known as Black Knight. Over the next few months, he learned of and developed his skills and powers. He developed the skills of the ninja. He now has the power to confuse or hypnotize. He has the power to teleport and to levitate. He has superhuman speed, strength, and endurance. He has powers to transform into dark creatures or monsters.

Fast forward to the present. One night, Black Knight hears a scream. He opens the window as he begins to transform into a werewolf. He smells blood and senses a type of force and power nearby. He wants that power. He growls and jumps through his window. Shattered glass fills through the air.

He quickly and quietly comes upon a man in a cloak and cowl, grasping a bloodied sword and a dying victim on the ground nearby. The cloaked man is V-Man.

"Grrrr!" Black Knight growls and lunges at V-Man.

"Oh no…" V-Man says.

Part 2-Origin of V-Man

A criminal mastermind named Casey Watts enjoyed exploring. One day, in the mountains, he came across something very interesting. Come to find out, it was a radioactive bomb. He had tampered with it and it had exploded. Miraculously, he had survived, even though he was covered in rubble.

The blast had given his superhuman strength. He broke out of the pile. He then learned ninja skills and became V-Man. Armed with his sword, claws, and shuriken, his ambitions grew.

Presently, he is stalking the night in the city when comes upon a man who was trying to protect his family after he had heard something outside. The man is carrying a knife. V-Man runs him through with his sword. The man screams in pain and terror.

V-Man hears a growl from behind and turns to see Black Knight, as a werewolf, who lunges at him.

Part 3-Origin of Ninja Warrior

A young ninja named Hata Yasuo was in the circus. He mastered the tight rope. He had excellent skills with swords and knives.

His father had fought in a secret underground MMA fighting ring. When one fighter killed another, the winner gained the powers of his opponent. The fighters had various skills, powers and abilities.

His father had a duel with a man called Flying Bear to the death and had lost. The young man cradled his father in his arms and watched him die.

The young ninja later avenged his father by killing Flying Bear. Learning mystical arts, he gained the power to fly, grow, and to have superhuman strength.

Now called Ninja Warrior, he prowls the streets to stop evil. One night he hears a scream, then some loud growling. He sees Black Knight attacking V-Man.

"Down boy!" V-Man yells as the werewolf lunges at him.

"Excuse me, gentlemen, but may I join in on the fun?" Ninja Warrior says.

With his sword, V-Man slashes across Black Knight's chest. Black Knight howls in pain.

Part 4-The Others

A man named Lindon Oliver had killed Super Ninja Kangaroo in the underground fighting ring. In doing this, he had acquired all the ninja's powers. He knew of V-Man, and while he felt that the villain was misguided on his morals, he liked him. He decided to call himself V-Man II. He is friends with Ninja Warrior and fights crime.

A man named Jackson Magog had killed Power Eel, which gave him powers as well. He is a dwarf (i.e. Midget, little person, etc.) Everyone had made fun of him, so he decided to get them back. He knows Black Knight, who is his friend and partner. He also knew of V-Man and V-Man II, so he decided to call himself V-Man III.

Cyrus Kelly had killed a powerful troll and had gotten his powers. He liked all the V-Mans, so he called himself V-Man IV. He knows the original V-Man best and is his partner. His weapons include swords, claws, mini missiles, and power capsules. His powers include: his blood and skin are like acid to others, he can grow and shrink, he has super strength, he can fly and has the skills of a ninja.

Elsewhere, a major and a general were in an experiment. The army gave them powers and weapons. The general called himself General Metal Tiger. He has a magical sword. He can also turn into a metal tiger, run very fast and has super strength. In addition to his arsenal of weapons, Major Mayhem has claws, can fly, had super strength, can turn into any other animal (he prefers his metal tiger form), and can shoot lasers from his hands and eyes.

Kirk Flynn killed Ghost Bird and had gained his powers but had lost an arm in the process. After recovering from the ordeal, he had received a robotic arm and weapons. He became Razor. He trained in acrobatics, which he had learned from the V-Man I, IV and V. He is V-Man V's partner.

Louis Kemp was searching some ruins when he had found a chest plate with symbols on it. He put it on and was transformed into an ancient Egyptian god.

These parties happened to come together serendipitously. And a battle broke out. They squared off, man against man.

Part 5-General Metal Tiger vs. V-Man IV

"I'm ready!" General Metal Tiger yells with authority.

"C'mon, punk!" screams V-Man IV.

The general runs quickly, in for the kill. He punches V-Man IV, who then slices with his claws. The general dodged, but it ripped his cape off.

General Metal Tiger fires a blast from his six-shooter and fires a blast from his mystical sword. But V-Man IV shrinks himself, so is able to dodge the blasts. V-Man IV grows back. The general blasts with both again, but the V-Man dodges.

V-Man IV picks up a boulder and throws it at the General. The general destroys it with his sword. V-Man IV throws explosive capsules and fires missiles from his bracelets. The V-Man then takes off his gloves and touches the general, who screams in pain and anguish, then dies.

Part 6-V-Man I vs. Major Mayhem

"Die!" V-Man screams in anger.

"C'mon!" the Major growls with determination.

V-Man hurls his shuriken at the major, who responds instantly by transforming into a giant armadillo and forms into an armored ball. The Chinese stars harmlessly bounce off his armored shell.

The major transforms back as V-Man flips in the air toward him. The major fires blasts from his hands, which V-Man dodges in midair and slices toward the major, but another blast by the major destroys his sword.

V-Man throws garbage cans at Major Mayhem, but the major blasts them out of the air. The major shoots flame out of his eyes after raising his visor, igniting V-Man's costume with the flames.

V-Man lays on the ground, smoke billowing from his body. Major Mayhem calmly walks toward him as he pulls out his Uzi. Is he dead? NO! He growls and lunges at Major Mayhem. Major Mayhem blasts away. Now he is (dead)!

Part 7-Black Knight vs. V-Man II

Black Knight teleports V-Man II's shuriken into the sewer. V-Man II throws knives, but the get teleported back to V-Man II, ripping off his cape.

"You're one ugly mother," quips Black Knight with a growl.

V-Man II raises his sword and growls ferociously as he attacks.

But he is badly injured because Black Knight slices off his hand with his chained scythe. V-Man groans as he tosses a bomb, which explodes and Black Knight dodges. V-Man II picks up a garbage can with his one good arm and throws it. It connects with Black Knight's chest. V-Man II runs. He tries to use his powers to jump over a building, but he is weakened and slams into the side of it and dies upon slamming into the ground after falling.

Part 8-Ninja Warrior vs. V-Man III

Ninja Warrior climbs onto a building. V-Man III follows by flying up. They are ready to fight. Just as the V-Man was shrinking, Ninja Warrior had thrown a shuriken, which hit the V-Man's utility belt and sent it flying off the building. V-Man III fires blasts from his hands, which the ninja easily dodges. Ninja Warrior, in turn, hurls three shuriken which get imbedded into the V-Man's arm, chest and leg.

V-Man III tosses a small bomb which Ninja Warrior dodges. They pull out their swords and simultaneously strike but break their swords. Ninja Warrior swiftly and stealthily hurls a dagger, which enters V-Man III's heart. The V-Man groans in pain and dies.

Part 9-Black Knight vs. V-Man IV

Black Knight uses his mind powers to confuse V-Man IV.

"Who am I? Where am I? What am I?" he mumbles.

Black Knight transforms himself into a beast as he causes V-Man IV to levitate, then claw himself. Black Knight then teleports V-Man IV into a volcano, where he dies in the lava.

Part 10-Major Mayhem vs. V-Man V

Major Mayhem fires his Uzi into the chest of V-Man V, but the bullets harmlessly bounce off his armor. The Egyptian laughs at the futility of the attempt.

Major Mayhem then blasts from his hand and from his eyes after lifting his visor. The blasts knock off the armor and helmet of the V-Man. The major then connects with a solid punch to the jaw of V-Man V, sending him flying into a dumpster. V-Man V escapes. Major Mayhem then flies after him.

V-Man V is hiding in a rural area on the outskirts of town, a hilly area with a small lake. His heightened sense of smell in his animal form picks up a scent.

That's funny…I sense something closing in fast…thinks V-Man V. Then he hears a noise from behind. Major Mayhem, in a creature form, had flown out of the water and toward V-Man V. MM punches V-Man V and sends him flying into a large rock. The

Major grabs the V-Man and is about to fire a blast with his eyes. But V-Man V fires a blast from his eyes, hitting MM in the chest.

MM fires from his guns while firing blasts from his eyes, critically injuring VM. MM leaves him for dead.

Part 11-Ninja Warrior vs. Razor

"C'mon!" growls Razor defiantly.

Razor throws spikes. Ninja Warrior knocks them away with his sword. NW slices and cuts off Razor's left hand. Razor creates a force field which blocks the next blade attack from NW. Razor then chokes Ninja Warrior with his telekinetic powers. NW breaks free, then makes a flying leap and slashes across Razor's chest, then punches him.

Part 12-Black Knight vs. V-Man V

V-Man V heals himself. He then teleports Black Knight's weapons away. Bearing his claws and with a charge of power, Black Knight then yells and flies toward VMV. VMV uses his power as well, the combination of which destroys them both, their smoking corpses lying on the ground.

Part 13-Ninja Warrior vs. Major Mayhem

Major Mayhem fires a blast from his hand, but Ninja Warrior dodges as he flies into the air toward his enemy, brandishing a blade. He swings and misses as Major Mayhem shrunk and changed into a possessed rat, flying in the air.

"DIE!" Major Mayhem the rat screams as he blasts from his eyes but misses.

Ninja Warrior slashes again, slicing across the creature's chest.

Major Mayhem changes back, a bloody slash across his chest.

"You will die!" Major Mayhem growls.

Ninja Warrior uses his power and grows to the size of a building.

"No. You will die!" he bellows.

Major Mayhem fires a blast but misses as NW shrinks back. MM fires a blast from his eyes, which destroys NW's blade. MM throws two garbage cans, but NW dodges. NW extends claws from his gloves and slices through MM's chest, killing him.

The END

The Beasts

It is an eerie, thunderous, fall night in a small town on the East Coast. Mist curls up through cracks in the sidewalks. A palpable silence hangs over the city. An old man breaks into the local zoo and lets some snakes and a bear loose, free to prowl the streets for food.

Next, the man swiftly enters the dog pound. He lets two pit bulls loose. As he walks away from the dog pound, the bear catches up with him. The bear roars in anger. It slashes the man's throat. It chomps down on the man's neck and rips out his jugular. Within moments, the bear reduces him to a quivering heap of torn and bloody flesh, lying on the sidewalk.

Minutes later, at a nearby cemetery, a grave digger is digging a grave. Due to budget cuts, he must do it with just a shovel. As he is shoveling, he hears a growl from behind. He turns and looks up at the massive bear. The bear swings its clawed paw at him. The gravedigger dodges, falling into the grave. The beast dives in after him and the man's panicked, muffled screams fill the air.

Meanwhile, nearby, Solomon Young, a 22-year-old policeman who fought in the Middle East, is down on his luck. His wife has left him. He awakens from a nightmare, a common occurrence as of late. He self-medicates with a small amount of whiskey.

"I'm sick of this crap. Life is just one problem, right after the other," he mutters as he downs the alcohol and grabs his 9mm, peering at it intently. "No one would miss me if I was gone," he continues gloomily.

A loud crash and some growling and screaming fills the air. Solomon peers out the window and sees the animals near his house. Corpses are strewn all over the place.

He quickly and quietly grabs his shotgun and pistol, along with a hand grenade.

The young man creeps out the back door of his home. He sees that the snakes are grouped together. He tosses the grenade across his yard. It lands in the middle of the snakes. Upon exploding, bits of snake fly everywhere.

Suddenly, behind him, Solomon hears a vicious growl. He turns to see the huge bear. Its black, dead eyes glare at him menacingly. He blasts it with his shotgun. Blood splatters as he blows the bears arm clean off. The bear lunges and claws the Solomon's leg with its other arm. Solomon fires his handgun. It hits the bear in the leg. It slams to the ground. He fires the shotgun again. The bear's head erupts in an explosion of skin, hair, skull, blood, and brains.

At a nearby house, a middle-aged man charges out his front door. Brandishing a handgun, he runs toward the vicious pit bulls to get a better shot. With uncanny speed, they charge toward him, then jump. The man's arms are torn from his body. Blood erupts from the stumps and blood foams from his mouth as he falls onto his back.

Alex runs over. He fires his shotgun. The head of one of the pit bulls flies through the air, still holding the arm of the unfortunate homeowner. The head and arm land near the other dog. The second dog drops the arm it was holding and charges toward Solomon. Without hesitating, Solomon fires his handgun, leaving a bullet hole in the middle of the dog's head. The dog falls. Blood trickles from the hole.

The young policeman calmly leaves the bloody carcasses and limps away as he calls in to the police station to tell them what had happened.

The END!

Air Ace

Along the California coast, a ship arrives at a hidden base.

"Yes, my lord?" says the pilot submissively as he kneels before his leader.

"You must destroy the enemy force without mercy, shape changer. Then, we will rule the world!" says the leader with determination.

"Yes, my lord!" says the shape changer abruptly.

Then they both laugh maniacally.

Meanwhile, in Utah, a new group of recruits arrive for training to be pilots. They see a group of injured men arriving from the battlefield, in bad shape.

Months later, Air Ace, the hotshot pilot from the group, has gotten to know others, including Goliath (a large fellow) and another pilot that has a pincer for a hand named Cam.

The three of them get in their jets and fly out. They attack an enemy air craft carrier and destroy it. They attack their next target but get shot down in the process.

Air Ace is with Cam. An enemy fires at them but misses. They take him out.

"Let's get out of here!" says Air Ace.

They see an enemy coming toward them on a small hovercraft, who starts firing.

They shoot the enemy, then take his vehicle. They see that an enemy base is nearby. They decide to attack, guns blazing. They are doing well, but suddenly, a large mech warrior with heavy weaponry emerges.

"Keep firing away!" Air Ace says to Cam.

BOOM! The large machine explodes.

Goliath and another pilot emerge from nearby foliage.

"Goliath! How you doin', man?" says Air Ace.

Before they can answer, they hear a loud squawk and look up to see a cyborg pterodactyl firing down at them. A blast hits Goliath's co-pilot, killing him.

The three shoot down the creature.

They find some enemy jet fighters. They head back to base, but just as Air Ace was trying to land, the opening had quickly closed because enemies were attacking. So, Air Ace goes out on his own.

He goes back to the enemy base and sneaks inside. He takes out a soldier on patrol. He makes it past some sensors. Then he sees another guard who is nodding off. He throws some small pieces of metal to distract the guard, then knocks him out.

He finds the electrical room. He takes out the guard. He sets a bomb with a timer. He finds a small jet and leaves just as the base is exploding.

As he is flying away, a mystical power takes over his ship, forcing him to crash land.

After he gets out, two dark figures materialize into view before him.

One is in an enemy soldier's uniform and the other is in a cloak.

"Think it's over?" whispers the cloaked figure in a raspy voice. "Use this!" he continues as he tosses Air Ace a small knife.

The enemy soldier pulls out his sword. The two attack simultaneously. Air Ace strikes the enemy's helmet while the soldier slashes across Air Ace's chest.

The soldier throws down his helmet. Air Ace kicks him across the face, punches him, then swiftly stabs him in the chest. Air Ace finishes off the soldier with a blast from his gun.

Air Ace hurls his knife and hits the cloaked figure in the face. The figure falls to the ground as if it were a puppet with its strings cut.

The figure then transforms into a small plane and starts firing at Air Ace. But Air Ace tosses a grenade, which blows up the creature.

Air Ace can get back to his base. Mission Accomplished!

The End

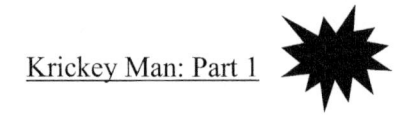

<u>Krickey Man: Part 1</u>

George "Krickey Man" Dundee was born in the Australian Outback in 1968. Until he was in his late teens, he was extremely interested in wild animals. He would study and watch them with great interest.

Later, he became interested in appliances. He became interested in them partially due to advances in science and technology. He had seen how new appliances were introduced and how they have evolved over time.

The other thing that interested him about appliances was when he was on a safari at age 21, he saw something very interesting. He was riding in his large SUV, when he saw wild appliances. He would eventually take people on "adventures" and watch these various types of wild creatures sneaking around. He saw vacuums sucking up dirt and rocks, wild fridges, washers, and dryers were roaming the land. The fridges, washers, and dryers would battle to take control of their territory.

Flying microwaves were also there. They would catch birds, then cook them and eat them. Wild dishwashers would lurk in the water, looking for dishes to clean. The smaller wild appliances, such as toasters, would stay in the jungle.

He met Krickey Mommy a few years later at a dance. She now joins him on his many adventures. She cares for Krickey Christian, Krickey Cameron, and Krickey Grant, their three children.

Krickey Christian is his right-hand man. Or his sidekick. He is very skilled at using their vehicles. He knows how to use the weapons and gadgets on the vehicles. He is very brave.

Krickey Cameron has superpowers. He can fly, has incredible strength, and speaks any language other than English.

Krickey Grant is excellent in archery. Due to his size, he is excellent at hiding and sneaking. Sometimes Krickey Man calls him Gremlin because he is so sneaky.

There is also Krickey Bob, who is the uncle. He is kind of a fly on the wall, so to speak. He helps as needed and is a mechanic. He knows appliances very well.

Thus, ends the introductory story of the Krickey team. Their further adventures will be explored in other stories, such as how the conflict began against the Connor team and about the study of appliances.

Part 2

Krickey. That is what George Dundee thought as he saw a huge explosion. The explosion was coming from a nearby appliance factory. Reacting quickly, he drove his bus over to the factory to investigate.

He drove closer then used his binoculars to see what was going on. He saw his former neighbor, Gary Connor, and his son, Mike. They were running from the scene. They had gotten into their van and had sped off.

Krickey Man followed them as he called the police. He tried not to get too close. But then the Connors saw him.

The Connor team turned so that the Krickey Man was driving toward the side of their van. Those inside threw open the side door of the van. Machine guns emerged. Shots rang out.

Krickey Man swerved to avoid the shots, but then drove the minivan off a nearby cliff. The van careened into a ravine. The Connors then drove to the edge of the cliff. There was a massive explosion, so they leave him for dead.

Krickey Man was holding onto a branch over the cliff, out of view. He had jumped out as the van was barreling over the edge of the cliff.

After the Connor team had left, George had pulled himself up.

The police soon showed up. Krickey Man told them everything. After much deliberation, the police referred him to a special department. They made him a specialist and gave him the resources to study appliances and to stop the Connor team. Over the next several months, they gave him access to advanced technology. He updated his new van with the new technology.

The Connor team found out about Krickey Man's new position. They decided to stop him. This was their new agenda, along with their chosen mission to destroy appliances and the environment.

Krickey Man realized that the Connor's trademark vehicles were large and used up a lot of gasoline. He has learned to always watch out for them. The Connors are always trying to stop him by whatever means necessary.

The End

SPACE STORIES
Kulos!
Kulos is a highly trained space soldier. His ship is flying through space. An enemy sees his ship from below. It locks on and fires its blasters, hitting his ship.

"Everyone to the escape pod!" Kulos yells while running.

Mass chaos ensues. He sees one of his men, an alien, running while on fire.

Minutes later, he and some men are in a smaller ship soaring away, but one of the enemy ships latches on, then boards their ship.

Armored robots enter the ship and start attacking. The men of Kulos try to defend themselves, but their attempts are futile.

Kulos swiftly throws on a space suit, then gets in a one-man escape pod. But he is captured again.

He is beat up, then thrown into a cell, being unconscious. He regains consciousness as an alien in the cell with him is going to assault him.

With a knee to the belly and a punch to the face, he knocks out his cellmate.

Surprisingly, he can escape through an air vent. After he emerges from the vent, a robot approaches, blaster raised.

"Stop!" it says.

He quickly rolls the food cart into the machine, then disables it.

Minutes later, he puts on parts of the robot to make it appear that he is a robot also.

A caped human sees him as he is walking down a corridor and says, "What happened?"

Kulos fires his blaster, vaporizing the man.

"Stop!" says another robot as it fires a beam from its chest.

The beam destroys the robotic exterior that he had on. Kulos fires his blaster, hitting the bot in the chest, putting it out of commission.

"Intruder!" Kulos hears from behind as another robot fires a blast from its chest, knocking him unconscious.

He is captured yet again, strapped to a wall and in chains. He snaps the chains from the wall, then is quickly able to get a gun from a guard, then shoot him in the throat.

A hulking, monstrous figure emerges from a nearby corridor and smashes the floor with his fists, knocking Kulos to the floor. Kulos shoots him in the throat.

Shortly thereafter, Kulos enters the hangar bay and escapes in a ship.

The End

Space Ninja

Space Ninja is part of a space force. Their enemies are the Birds of Prey. The Birds of Prey are dressed as birds, their ships are shaped like birds, and they are as merciless as birds of prey.

Space Ninja is flying through space when he comes upon a large Bird of Prey ship. He fires and hits the hull.

Bad move, he thinks as the larger ship sends a flurry of blasts at him. His wing is hit, and his ship begins to spin out of control. He ejects and is in his ninja space suit. He stealthily flies up to the ship and slices his way in.

The pressure regulates as he enters the interior. Sirens are blaring. Two bird men approach, carrying weapons. Space Ninja acts quickly. With his blazing sword and his dagger, he uses a flurry of slashes to defeat his foes.

The End

Spaced-Out with Thrasher

In the distant future, Thrasher, a space warrior, in his ship, shoots out of his main ship, emerging from the mouth of a larger ship that has an opening like a face. It soars through space and comes upon a group of enemy ships.

ZOT! Thrasher fires his blaster and destroys a ship. One of the ships fires at Thrasher. BOOM! It destroys his ship. At the last second, Thrasher has ejected from his ship.

Wearing a space suit that includes a jet pack, he soars toward the enemy ship while igniting his laser sword. He slashes the windshield, then shatters it with a mighty punch.

Undetected, he reaches a large enemy ship. He cuts his way in with his sword.

But a large robot in armor, named Horne, blasts him and he explodes into hundreds of pieces.

The END

<u>Phaser</u>
Phaser is a special ops agent in space. He and his partner have infiltrated an enemy ship. They are discovered by an enemy

guard, who then fires a blast that blasts his partner's chest, killing him.

"Nooo!" Phaser screams, then fires his blaster, blowing the guard's head apart.

Phaser decides to avenge his friend.

Another guard enters the room. Phaser fires a blast that enters through both thighs of the guard, hitting major arteries.

Phaser changes his uniform. He now has two swords.

Unbeknownst to him, a savage enemy with a mohawk sees him from above. The enemy grabs some thick electrical wire, then swings down. The enemy kicks Phaser's blaster out of his hand, then punches him as he says, "Darketo curse you!"

Phaser slashes across the enemy's chest with his claws.

The enemy knocks Phaser's mask off, then punches him in the face.

The enemy grabs Phaser's blaster and fires as he says, "Die Phaser!"

The blast rips through Phaser, his innards splatting against the wall.

The End

Executioner

Executioner was, well, an Executioner, to say the least. And his enemy, Executioner II, wanted to be the only Executioner. So, he met with his men.

"Kill Executioner and Dog Man!" he said.

Dog Man was Executioner's side kick.

"Yeah, boss," says a large gorilla man that had a small winged creature on his shoulder.

"Me too?" says a large frog man.

"Yeah, sure," says Executioner II.

Later, the two henchmen track down Dog Man and he is alone.

"Hasta la vista, baby!" said the frog man.

"Huh?" said Dog Man in surprise.

The small creature flies toward Dog Man. It squawked as Dog Man punched it and killed it in mid-air.

Frog Man leaped with his powerful legs and smashed Dog Man to the pavement, a cracking noise filling the air, killing him instantly.

Minutes later, Executioner came upon the carnage. Written in Dog Man's blood, it said: II's gang was here…YOU'RE NEXT!!

"Noooo!" screamed Executioner.

Executioner then found out where Executioner II's base was. But as he neared it, the two henchmen were in a small ship and fired down upon him. They missed.

But Executioner fired a missile from his arm and destroyed the ship. He then continued to the base and destroyed it with all his ammo. As he was leaving, there was a massive rockslide and a boulder crushed him from above, killing him instantly. THE END

Fire-Bots and Hock-Man: Fightin' Crime!

The Fire-Bots consist of six robots who fight crime. Punk is a street-smart bot that is a master of knives. Flame is a master of flame. Crusher is very strong. Wheels is a wheeled machine. Cool has the power to create cold, such as snow, hail or ice. Chill is like a gang member and likes machine guns.

The bots come upon a man wielding a rocket launcher. Before they can react, Crusher, Wheels, and Chill are blown up by one of the man's rockets.

Suddenly, the man is enveloped in a blast of power and he changes.

"Behold! I am Skull Bot!" he screams at the other bots, then transforms into a gun wielding bot.

Punk forcefully charges toward him, but Skull Bot fires his gun, hitting Punk in the head. He explodes, killing both of them.

Seconds later, another opponent appears. It is a large bot that has rocket launchers attached to its shoulders and one arm is a rocket launcher.

"MUST KILL FIRE-BOTS!" it says in its robotic voice as it fires a barrage of missiles at Cool, destroying him.

"NOOO!" Flame screams robotically. Realizing that his chances of survival were at a minimum, he flies upward in a column of flame.

"LAUNCHER PREVAILS!' says the bot with rockets.

Meanwhile, in the same city, a man named Joe Evans can transform into Hock-Man, a master of martial arts. He normally wears a hockey mask.

Joe comes upon a man with a sword and shield.

For no reason at all, the man yells at him, "Die you fool!"

Joe changes into Hock-Man and punches the man across the face, causing his enemy to lose his sword. Hock-Man grabs the sword from the air and runs through his enemy with the sword.

Suddenly, Flame lands near him.

"Help me!" the robot says.

Launcher lands a few dozen feet away, flying in with jets. Launcher fires a barrage of missiles, killing Flame and Hock-Man.

The END

Warriors of Justice vs. Death Squad

Far away, on a distant planet, there are two opposing groups.

The Warriors of Justice consists of three men. Nemesis and Livewire are muscular, seasoned soldiers who equip themselves with heavy firepower. GhostKnight dresses in white, with a cape and prefers to use various blades and melee weapons. Sai is a ninja that has mastered the Sai, his weapon of choice.

Their enemies are the Death Squad. Their leader, Cyber, is a huge, muscled man. He looks like an executioner, wearing all black including a mask. Ute is large as well. He is Native American and dresses in bright colors. He has super strength and has increased senses. Manslaughter is a monstrous demon. This clawed monster can produce weapons out of his body, typically spikes and blades. They lead a group of seasoned soldiers.

Death Squad went to the base of operations of the Warriors of Justice and started to attack. Ute begins the fight with a fierce war cry.

Livewire fires one of his guns and it his Cyber in the jaw. Blood erupts from the wound upon contact. Cyber lets out a bubbly scream as he hits the ground.

Nemesis guns down a few of the soldiers.

GhostKnight leaps toward Ute, and kicks him in the chest, sending Ute sprawling into space due to his incredible strength. Ute uses his powers to survive the vacuum of space. He sneaks onto a spaceship, hijacks it, and heads back to earth.

As Nemesis and Livewire run for cover, GhostKnight finishes off Cyber with his scimitar by beheading him.

Manslaughter sneaks up behind GhostKnight and rips his throat apart! Livewire tries to shoot Manslaughter, but hits GhostKnight instead. His dead body falls to the dirt.

High above, Ute leaps from the ship.

Livewire yells out for Nemesis to look out for Manslaughter as he fires at the villain. Nemesis is firing at the soldiers. He hears Livewire's yell, but was it in time? Unfortunately, no. But our hero (Nemesis) is not wounded.

Shedding some spikes, Manslaughter fires them at Nemesis. Nemesis is hit in the shoulder, side, and calf. He falls on his side.

"Huff!" exclaims Manslaughter as he is kicked in the back by Sai.

Livewire fires at Ute. The lasers and bullets bounce off.

The planet suddenly explodes.

The End

Planet of Death

It is the year 2030.... a large assault vehicle drives up to a building. A gun fires from the front of the vehicle and hits a man. He falls to the ground.

"Hurry up, guys!" a large armored man harshly whispers to two mutants as they grab the body.

Another man, a cyborg in a trench coat, is with him.

Elsewhere, shortly later, Speed Tiger, one of our heroes, slams the wall with his fist as he says, "Crime...it never decreases. We need to stop it."

Mike (their firearms and technology expert) and Powerstar (the mystic) are with him, watching the footage of the crime.

Minutes later, Mike sees another crime and records the footage on his camera. The cyborg lifts a screaming man as he fires a gun into his abdomen.

Later, Mike shows the footage.

"See? Everyone with me?" Speed Tiger asks the others.

"Yeah, sure!" Mike and Powerstar yell.

Shortly after, Speed Tiger patrols the streets, looking for trouble.

A mutant, one that Speed Tiger has been wanting to take down, is walking down the street and humming. The last sound coming from his mouth is a yell as Speed Tiger's extremely sharp claws rip through him.

Speed Tiger wraps the criminal up in his cape and puts him with the trash.

Seconds later, another mutant comes walking nearby. Speed Tiger quickly climbs the wall in the shadows.

"That was Tavros's...SCREAM!" the mutant yells as he sees Speed Tiger descending from above.

On a nearby street, a cloaked man is walking by the cyborg.

"Excuse me." Says the cloaked man to the cyborg as he walks by.

"Eat this!" the cyborg yells as he whips out his heavy-duty machine gun and fires at the stranger.

The stranger is Powerstar. He deflects the bullets back at the cyborg with a force field. The cyborg gasps in pain as the bullets slam into him. Powerstar picks up the machine gun.

Elsewhere, a boombox blasting hard rock fills the air as it rests on a shadowy figure's shoulder.

Some mutant screams, "Turn down the boombox!"

Mike, holding the boombox, presses a button on it. It fires a missile that explodes upon hitting the mutant, pieces flying in all directions.

A costumed villain emerges from a nearby manhole.

"Ha!" he says as he rises from the hole.

Mike fires another missile. It imbeds into the villain's chest, then explodes. Mike descends into the sewer. Recording on his camera, he finds evidence that people and mutants are being experimented upon.

A werewolf-type creature comes into view, growling at him. Mike fires his gun into its chest. It growls in pain.

Mike is calmly walking past the prone creature, when it grabs his leg. Mike fires two shots, one in the foot and one in the head. Upon impact, the creature transforms back into a human and his last words are a groan in pain.

Meanwhile, Speed Tiger has taken his last enemy's leather jacket and his gun. He hears panicked yelling from above. He sees a large being holding a man above his head.

"Put him down!" Speed Tiger yells.

"OK." says the large man as his throws the man off the building.

Speed Tiger fires into the large man's chest and continues to fire as the man dives from the building toward him.

The large man slams into the pavement, split seconds after Speed Tiger has dived out of the way. Speed Tiger fires again into the man's chest. He must be superhuman or has some type of powerful armor, he thinks to himself.

Yelling out of annoyance, the man punches Speed Tiger and sends him flying into a garbage can.

"He flattened me," Speed Tiger whispers in disbelief, blood dripping from his nostrils.

Determined to finish this, Speed Tiger unleashes a barrage of bullets into the man's head and chest. The large man falls. Speed Tiger throws his helmet at the corpse in frustration.

Elsewhere, Powerstar's gun is blasted out of his hand from behind. As he is turning around, his robe is engulfed in flames. He throws the robe to the ground.

He sees a massive lizard man dressed in jeans and a leather jacket, a smoking gun in hand. The lizard, named Flogg, hisses at him.

Flogg hisses again as it blasts Powerstar in the chest. Powerstar grunts in pain as he dies.

Simultaneously, Mike is blasted by a mysterious villain and Speed Tiger is blasted in the chest by a large-headed mutant named Bulge. Both collapse and are left for dead. But they recover.

"I can't believe that Powerstar died," says Mike. "We were lucky to recover."

"I know, man," says Speed Tiger.

Suddenly, Mike is shot from behind, through the chest. He groans and then dies.

"Mike!" Speed Tiger yells in fury as he charges toward the enemy.

BLAM! Another blast from the gun hits Speed Tiger in the chest and he dies as well.

"She-Man triumphs again!" the transgendered villain screams in victory.

The END!

Bi-Leap

Bi-Leap is a superhero. He is a pro at using mountain bikes, acrobatics, and he can jump long distances. His gear includes sunglasses and a suit with a logo that has 2 triangles.

Gary Connor, an ex-con, decides that he wants Bi-Leap as his next victim. Armed with an Uzi and a 9mm, he suddenly charges toward Bi-Leap.

The warden of the prison suddenly appears, so Connor blows him away instead.

Moving quickly, Bi-Leap tosses his bike to the side and leaps the other way as Connor attempts to pump his guts full of lead.

Connor barely misses! Bi-Leap is twisting and turning in the air, barely staying in front of the bullets.

Bi-Leap summersaults over to Connor. He kicks Connor squarely in the chest. The 50-year old huffs a bunch of air and sprawls backwards. He drops his Uzi. Bi-Leap picks it up and starts spraying bullets into the night air.

Connor howls in pain as bullets hit him multiple times. He is hit in the shoulder, side, and upper leg. Connor then opens fire. Bullets hit him in the hand and foot as he attempts to dodge.

Bi-Leap uses his remaining strength to pick up his bike and pedal away. He manages to get around a corner but is hit by a dump truck traveling at full speed because the driver wasn't watching where he was going.

His bloody guts are sucked into the fan and chopped up into little pieces.

Prologue-Connor died from gangrene infection.

The End

The Murder of Big Dan

Jim and I found Big Dan's body face down in the river. A knife with an ivory handle was in his back. I pulled it out of his back.

"George," said Jim, "Who do you think murdered him, and why?"

"I think some rich men did. Maybe whoever it was might have been mad because they had lost a bet with him," I said as I put the knife in my belt.

I heard something. I turned around. There were about 30 mountain men holding weapons.

"Of course, we killed him!" a man growls. The grizzled mountain man was wearing black furs and had red hair and a red beard.

"He called me a yellow-bellied liar when I caught him cheating during a card game. Now you two are going to join him in death. Attack!" he continued with a scream.

I had to think quickly, so I pulled out my rifle and had shot at a large branch above them. It was a perfect shot. The branch fell on some of the men.

Jim and I started running across the river. While I was running, my rifle was in the way, so I threw it and tried to hit one of the mountain men. The rifle hit one of them right in the face! He fell and knocked over a couple of his friends.

We were running for about ten minutes, when all the sudden, I saw a snake. It was about 10 feet in front of me. It was about 19 feet long. I think that it was a diamondback rattler. I looked back. Our pursuers were about 30 feet behind me. There were about 18 of them.

We each threw our knives. We each hit some. We then threw our tomahawks. We each hit a man. After throwing the weapons, we ran around the snake.

A few of the men were afraid of the snake and ran away.

The remaining mountain men caught up to us. We fought fiercely. We won and had barely escaped with our lives.

THE END

MYTHS
The Myth of Volcanoes

Flara (the goddess of fire), Aquarious (the water god) and Gaya (the earth goddess) wanted to tell the secrets of the gods to the people of Earth. Shradious (the god of shadows) heard of this. He quickly told Hegadious (the god of gods) about this. Hegadious became very angry. He sent Lapious (the god of justice) to catch them. He was successful. Lapious brought the three to Hegadious.

"You three know that it isn't right to tell those pitiful humans our secrets," yelled Hegadious. "You will be punished for your plan."

Flara, Aquarious, and Gaya were sent to the center of the earth as their punishment.

Flara tried to use her fire to escape, but the earth wouldn't burn.

Aquarious used his water to make an opening in the earth so he could escape, but mud started falling because the water made mud out of the earthen soil.

Gaya made some holes in some mountains with her powers.

The three would have tried to fly out of the holes, but Hegadious had taken away their flying abilities.

"Maybe if we combine our powers, we can get out," said Aquarious.

They all mixed together their powers. Gaya's soil and Aquarius's water became mud. Flara added fire. The mud became red and very hot. This mud is called lava.

To this day, they now shoot it up through the holes in the mountains to try to get out. They would escape, but they don't have enough time because they can't make lava and climb out at the same time as they must use their powers to make the lava.

The lava blasts out of the mountains which are called volcanoes because the three had made so much lava and blasted it out of the volcanoes with so much force. And therefore, we have volcanoes.

The End

The Myth of the Bermuda Triangle

This myth is about the Bermuda Triangle. The Bermuda Triangle is near Florida. Those involved were Hades, Ares, Zeus, Poseidon, Medusa the gorgon, Hercules, the furies, Charon and Oresius.

Oresius was the god of space. He had, like Zeus, the power of thunderbolts. He also had the space sword. His symbol was the eye, because he could see the entire earth at the same time.

One day Hades, Medusa, 15 furies, Ares, Charon and Oresius were meeting together. They planned to prepare a surprise for any who tried to get to North America. Zeus heard of the plan. He had sent Poseidon and Hercules after them. Hercules traveled in a ship.

Upon arrival, Hercules pulled out his bow and arrows. He shot down 10 of the furies. Hades used his cloak of darkness so that he couldn't be seen. Oresius disappeared. The furies picked up Medusa and hid behind some rocks. Charon steered his boat out of combat. Oresius battled Poseidon and Ares battled Hercules. Poseidon tried to stab Oresius with his trident but missed. Oresius became extremely angry. He hurled a bolt of thunder at Poseidon, which hit its mark. It gave him a horrible headache. Poseidon left because he was in too much pain.

Meanwhile, Ares shrank to the size of Hercules and jumped onto Hercules's ship. Ares pulled out his sword. Because he was the god of war, he was an excellent swordsman. Hercules pulled out his sword as well. A fierce and vicious sword fight commenced. Ares sliced Hercules's right arm. Hercules grasped his arm and asked for his father's help.

Zeus appeared. He picked Hercules up and healed him. Zeus then took him to his home and hurled a thunderbolt at Ares, who was still in the ship. The ship exploded upon impact. Ares quickly and quietly left and went back to Olympus.

Hades left his cloak of darkness in the sky, above the Bermuda Triangle.

To this day, these gods always watch for people who go into the triangle. Sometimes Poseidon smashes the sea floor with his fists which cause strong waves all over the world. Sometimes Oresius throws his thunderbolts into the triangle and summons alien ships from different planets into the triangle. The cloak of darkness and the thunderbolts form storms that occur in the triangle.

Medusa lurks in the triangle's waters. If people look into her eyes, they turn into stone and ships are lost at sea. The 5 furies fly around in the triangle. They attack people with their metal-studded whips and work people up into committing suicide.

Charon picks up the souls of those who have died when he has a little bit of time to spare. He lets their ships and planes sink to the bottom of the ocean.

This explains how the Bermuda Triangle was formed, why ships and planes are lost at sea, why there are storms and currents, and why there may be alien ships there, how people die, and how the bodies are never found.

The End

The 13th Labor of Hercules

This is the story of the 13th labor of Hercules. He had to do battle with Vilocious and his 50 men. Hercules only had 30 men.

Vilocious had better weapons and is bigger than Hercules. He was a cyclops. He had four fingers on each hand and a Mohawk.

Hercules and his men defeated all 50 of the men under Vilocious. After many hours of fighting, Hercules and Vilocious were the only ones left.

Hercules had hit Vilocious with ten of his arrows. Vilocious was angry. He then punched Hercules, who then flew about 20 feet, then slammed into a rock.

Vilocious then ran over to Hercules and spit in his face. He then picked him up, then threw him about 40 feet. Hercules landed on his back.

Hercules quickly draws his sword. Vilocious grabbed his large battle axe that was strapped to his back. Vilocious swung and missed with the massive weapon. Hercules then stabbed Vilocious in the stomach with his sword. Vilocious fell and died.

THE END!

Baldness and Aging-A Native American Myth

One night, there was a massive storm. There was thunder, lightning, and rain. Stealing Fox was making a spear in his teepee. He was wearing a buffalo skin to keep him dry and warm.

Suddenly, a lightning bolt struck his teepee, causing it to start on fire. Just as the lightning had struck, he had finished his spear. Quickly, he left the teepee with his spear before he got burned by the flames.

He had no food. He had no shelter. He was hungry and getting very wet.

He saw Running Chicken's tent. It was perfectly fine. He walked over to the teepee. He looked inside. He saw Running Chicken sleeping amongst his many skins. There was also plenty of food.

Stealing Fox swiftly and firmly stabbed Running Chicken many times with his spear. Running Chicken was dead, in a sleep in which he would never awake.

Stealing Fox cackled with glee because of the food and furs. But the earth god had heard his laughter.

The next morning, before any others in the tribe were awake, Stealing Fox was hiding Running Chicken's body behind some bushes and under some branches, away from the other teepees.

"You are guilty of killing Running Chicken, Stealing Fox! I saw you last night." The earth god yelled while he was trying to hide the body.

"I will make you lose all of the hair on your head. It is called baldness. I will also make you have wrinkles and you will have a weaker body as you become older. This is called age. Now because of you, people will lose the hair on their heads, and they will get wrinkles and weaker bodies as they get older. Leave this place and bury Running Chicken's body, you fool." The earth god said.

Stealing Fox buried the body and left the area. Stealing Fox was never seen again because of the curse of baldness, old age, and wrinkles. Because of that curse, people still have these curses today.

The End

IF

If I were born with three legs and long orange dreadlocked hair…

One day, there was an earthquake that was destroying the planet where we were from. My father was a scientist and he had built a spaceship for our family, so we came to earth, Salt Lake City, Utah to be exact.

There was nothing as strange about the rest of my family. But I was born with three legs and strange, orange hair. They didn't care that I was different, but they kept me hidden.

Over time, I had realized that my quirks had given me supernatural abilities.

I had snuck outside and found out that I could leap great distances and that my hair would make anything rust that touched it.

One day, I was walking down the street and a man said, "It's not Halloween, you know!"

"Oh…Er…umm…I'm going to a costume party." I stuttered.

I then bought a hat at a nearby store.

Further down the street, I saw a thief carrying a TV set. I then jumped to him, took off the hat, then made him touch my hair.

"Hey kid…watch…" he yelled.

Then there was a creaking sound. He was rusting! Before the TV owner could come to thank me, I jumped away from him.

As I jumped away, I then saw a car coming toward me. I jumped out of the way, but it started to follow me. I jumped onto a house, then jumped into a tree. I had lost my pursuers.

Then I went home. I saw the news on TV. The news anchor said: "Boy seen with three legs and strange hair in Salt Lake City, Utah!"

A man across the street saw me in my front room and shot at me. The bullet barely missed me. I then jumped over to him, dodging additional bullets.

I touched his gun with my hair, then punched him in the face. He fell to the ground.

Then I jumped around for a while.

Later, I saw some robots coming toward me. I jumped up high in the air, came down and smashed the head of one of the robots with my feet. Then the robots surrounded me, holding hands.

I touched one of the robots with my hair. They all rusted and blew up as I jumped out of their circle.

Lesson learned. I decided to lay low and not leave the house anymore.

The End

A Wild, Crazy, Scary Adventure

Kool is a man that has superpowers: He has super strength, can fly and can shoot lasers from his hands.

His worst enemy, Zoral, can make traps, shoot fire/ice/web walls, can run at high speeds, and has keen eyesight.

One day, Kool was dozing off on his sofa, when his video phone rang. He pushes the talk button.

"What do you want?" he yells as Zoral's face appears on the screen.

"You don't know?" Zoral asks. "Don't you want to stop by my haunted castle?" He cackles maniacally.

"Okay, I will." Kool says.

"Ha. Ha. You're smart." Zoral says.

Moments later, Kool activates his teleporter as he knows the approximate location and it is far away.

Kool is then transported to a gloomy and creepy forest. While he is treading along, he sees a huge werewolf with long, sharp, shiny talons and teeth. It lunges at Kool, but Kool flies out of the way.

Kool then shoots some nearby trees and they fall onto the werewolf. It growls and claws at the trees but can't get them off.

Kool flies off to look for the haunted castle. Suddenly, some giant birds are gliding toward him.

POW! He punches one in the beak. It falls into the trees. Then he finishes off the rest of the birds.

He sees the castle and soars toward it. He smashes through the door. An armored skeleton with a sword and a shield comes out of a nearby doorway and staggers toward him.

Kool punches the shield and it shatters.

ZAP! Kool blasts the skeleton and it blows apart. Then, out from the smoke, comes Zoral.

"The final battle!" Zoral exclaims through laughter. He creates a web shield. Kool blows it apart. "Ha!" yells Zoral as he runs away.

"Next time, Kool, next time," he laughs.

The End

The Ghost

John Maddock had died tragically. He went parachuting, but the parachute was sabotaged by a corrupt politician, William

Rhodes. He became the Ghost, who wreaks death upon all the evil and corrupt.

His first target is Mr. Rhodes. He travels to the home of the politician and enters through the wall. He finds Mr. Rhodes and comes at him with his short sword.

"Remember me?" the Ghost inquires.

The daughter, Chauncey, sees the apparition and starts to shriek. Mr. Rhodes's hand is then severed from his arm in one swift movement.

"Leave, you nuisance!" the Ghost roars as he fires at the girl with his 9mm handgun and intentionally misses, aiming above her head. She screams and runs, arms flailing.

"You will die for your corruption!" the Ghost bellows as William is crawling away, blood covering the floor.

"Not so fast." The Ghost whispers.

A few secret service men charge into the room. They try to grab the Ghost, but they go right through him and fall on the floor, knocking the breath out of themselves. They get up, gasping for air. The ghost fires 6 rounds into each man.

"Now for you!" the Ghost shouts at Mr. Rhodes.

"Mommy!" William squeals as he crawls under his desk.

The Ghost hauntingly stalks after him.

William's assistant enters the room.

"Did I come at a bad time?" he asks as he backs up.

"Freedom! That's the spirit, get it?" says the Ghost as he points his gun at Mr. Rhodes and fires into each hand, each thigh, and each eye.

As a final act, the Ghost enters the body of Mr. Rhodes and begins to flail and flop around.

Blood spurting, Mr. Rhodes moans until he dies shortly after. The body is now lifeless, and blood covers the floor.

The Ghost, having finished his dark work, leaves the body of Mr. Rhodes and disappears into another dimension.

The End…for now

Mighty Heroes in Training

Stone Wolf leads a small group, called the Mighty Heroes. Rad and Masked Avenger are present.

"Death Castle was hard," says Stone Wolf about his recent mission.

"Yeah, man?" says Rad. "Being a superhero is hard."

"I avenged my parents, but it was like trying to climb Mount Everest," says Masked Avenger.

"Okay, men! Training!" interrupts Stone Wolf as he barges into the room.

"All right!" says Rad enthusiastically.

Rad begins his training. He rides his special skateboard. He fires his 9mm and hits a target. A robot emerges from a doorway. He fires and hits it. He then clears a jump over a pit.

Masked Avenger is next. He sees a stun grenade flying toward him. He dives into a trench to avoid the blast. He fires with his machine gun, hitting a target. He dodges some projectiles, then some rubber bullets that were fired at him. He dives across a pit that is filled with several savage reptiles at the bottom.

Then there is Stone Wolf. A platform emerges from the floor in the training room, bringing him to the surface. He is surrounded by mannequins that fire rubber bullets from their guns. He dodges the blasts. Then, in a flurry of action, he takes out the mannequins by punching, kicking, and clawing them out of commission.

As he is finishing his training, a figure smashes through the wall. A man in a Bird of Prey suit emerges from the rubble. The Birds of Prey have been wreaking havoc on the city.

"Birds…attack!" the birdman screams as a large group of birdmen enter the training room as security alarms filling the air.

"Ha! Ha! A fight! Come on!" Stone Wolf laughs as he rips apart one of the birdmen with his long, razor-sharp claws.

He then continues his rampage with swift and brutal attacks, the birdmen flying in all directions from his blows and slashes.

Rad and Masked Avenger break down the door and run into the room. They fire away with their guns, taking out the remaining birdmen.

After the battle, Rad decides to leave because he was part of another group.

"Guys, they need me," Rad proclaims as he leaves the base.

A day later, the others hear that Rad was killed.

There is a knock at the door. It is a hero, named Pow, that wants to join the team. He is a tall and muscular man dressed in a basketball uniform. A spiked basketball on a chain dangles from his hand.

Suddenly, bullets fly. The new guy shoves Stone Wolf out of the way, saving his life. Simultaneously, Pow swings his weapon and hits a zombie wielding a machine gun, knocking its head off. Come to find out, it was a robot.

The team composes themselves and realize that the Strike Force was behind the attack. The Birds of Prey are led by Strike Force. Strike Force is a group of villains that have technologically advanced weapons. Throwing caution to the wind, the Mighty Heroes decide to make a preemptive strike and attack. In their stealth jet, they leave the U.S. and head to Germany.

Hours later, in a mountainous region, they see a member of the Strike Force. They fire a missile, blowing him up. This begins their assault. Days later, they have systematically eliminated the rest of Strike Force. The End

The Student

One day, a teacher is teaching a class. But suddenly, he screams, "NOOO!" and turns into a monstrous creature.

A courageous student gets up and draws a knife.

He turns and yells, "Get out!" to the other students.

But the teacher swiftly snaps his pointing stick over the students head, knocking him out.

The student slowly awakens to find himself tied up.

"You've been hog-tied…" growls the demon, "and you're going to be cooked like one too!"

The student breaks free.

"I don't think so. C'mon!" he defiantly shouts as he punches the demon in the head. "I don't play that, and I don't need no education!" he quips.

The demon quickly grabs him in a bear hug and squeezes. The student head-butts the demon, causing it to drop him. The student reaches for the knife and grabs it. He decapitates the demon, then tosses the head.

The END

Veterans

The night was dark and dreary. Harley Dawson had his M-16 in his lap. He heard some Vietnamese approaching. He quickly and quietly pulled out a grenade. He pulled out the pin and threw it at the soldiers.

BOOM!

All of them are dead now, he thought. But he was wrong. One of them had hid.

BRAT-TAT-TAT! The hiding soldier had shot him. Harley then hit the ground. He was dead. His fellow soldiers killed the soldier that had killed him.

***

Harley then found himself in a city with old and destroyed buildings. He was wearing different clothes and had had a gun. There were many warriors fighting each other.

He saw a mean looking punk with a gun. He quickly pulled the trigger on his gun. The bullet hits the punk in the neck, blood spurting out. The punk screamed and hit the ground.

Harley looked around in amazement, seeing much violence and destruction.

In front of him, he saw a tall man with long claws. He shoved his claws into a solder, then picked him up with the claws sticking out of his back.

Another punk ran toward Harley, magic swirling around his hands. A soldier shot the punk through the chest. Harley then saw a monster throwing a ball out of a lacrosse-type stick. The ball hit a building and exploded.

A motorcyclist fired shots at a lizard creature and hit it in the tail. A man from the damaged building fired and hit the lizard man in the eyes. A robot also fired at the lizard and hit it.

There was a man on a large lizard that was shooting at monsters. A giant ship shot at him but did not hit him. The ship then shot at a man with a laser and hit him.

A soldier punched a punk in the face. Two other soldiers fired at monsters and punks. A punk ripped through a man's chest with a claw.

The ship was there to take over. It shot at Harley and hit him. Everything went black.

The END

The Drug War

Quaid was trying to get away from the drug fighters because he was a drug dealer. He had his handgun ready. They almost had him. He had to think of something. He was surrounded.

The drug fighters had much better weapons than he did. They stared at him. A drug fighter fired at Quaid. Quaid fired at the same time. Quaid's arm flied off and hit the wall, splattering blood everywhere. Quaid screamed and had gotten away. The drug fighter lied dead on the floor with a bullet in his forehead. The other drug fighter had to check on his partner that got hit, so Quaid managed to get away successfully.

Quaid found his friend, Whizz. Whizz fixed him up and gave him a robotic arm. Quaid also now had a new armored suit. It was made of plate mail armor. His new gun was an awesome, powerful weapon. It was the best that he had ever seen. He loved it. He had tested it and it had worked perfectly. He now called himself Destructor.

Destructor went to the police station and entered. A police officer walked up with a nightstick. Without thinking, Destructor blasted away. After hitting a wall, the officer had become a hunk of smoking flesh after Destructor stopped firing. A lady that witnessed it had thrown up then fainted.

The cops kept on coming. And Destructor kept firing away. The room was smoking and full of blood and dead bodies.

Meanwhile, Joe Johnson, a very loyal policeman, knew what he had to do. He had to risk his life. He drove straight into the police station and started firing his gun. Destructor was caught off-guard. He got bombarded by several bullets after he was hit by the speeding car. Both Destructor and Joe were killed…The END

The Battle Over Ice Station Cobra

Ice Station Cobra was deep in Antarctica. The brutal temperatures kept it hidden. A group of radicals called Doaolkta, had it as their base of operations. There they would do mining and research that was used to further their cause of building an army to gain power.

Their enemies, a group called Zorrko, had worked against them, mainly sabotaging their machines.

One day, a spy came across the hidden station.

Our unnamed spy whispered, "Holy cow!" under his breath as he saw tents and other structures, as well as snow vehicles.

As he stood in amazement on a large, nearby hill, he became visible to a guard.

"Intruder!" the guard yelled as he fired upward toward the spy.

"Oh crap!" the spy said as he ran over the top of the hill, bullets pounding the hill behind him.

He tripped, then slid forward on his belly. As he increased speed, he saw a large hole at the bottom of the hill. As he slid down the hole, snow and ice covered his path. He landed in a pile of snow.

"I must be in some sort of station," he whispers.

Meanwhile, up above, two enemy fighter planes soar up above, looking for him. One plane has the name "Thrasher" on it and the other says "POW".

"No signs from here. Over," Said the Thrasher pilot.

Down below, a robot comes upon the spy.

"Who are you?" it says its robotic voice. The spy does not respond to the inquiry.

"You O.K.?" it says.

"Yeah," says the spy.

Up above, the fighters decide to quickly destroy the base after it is evacuated. They drop several bombs and it is destroyed.

The End!

The Hidden War

There is a war going on, including fierce battles. The US Army is putting up a fight. In one battle, a soldier is in the trenches. A weird looking man comes up from behind and asks for help.

"Stop! Please!" the man chants.

Then suddenly, the man explodes. The man was a robot that self-destructed.

A secret Neo-Nazi group has been causing destruction and chaos. However, their base had been infiltrated by a courageous soldier. The soldier finds out that the secret army is creating robots that are explosive.

He finds a leader of the group speaking to those under him as they work. He hurls explosives, then fires into the group with his machine gun. He escapes, having stopped the group in its tracks.

Meanwhile, mutant monsters are another threat. The monsters have a group of pilots called the Air Elite. This squadron confidently flies out to attack the US Air Force.

But the top pilot is out for maneuvers when the Air Elite show up in his systems.

"Somethin's comin!" he yells into his radio, then locks on to the lead ship and fires his most powerful missile, obliterating the enemy jet.

The enemy fires back, barely hitting him with their guns.

But with his excellent skills, he can take out all but one. The last remaining stealthily flies back to base, but the pilot has followed. He bombs the base, destroying it.

The End

###

About the Author

I was born and raised in Salt Lake City, Utah. My writing experience comes from my schooling, up through my bachelor's degree in Communication, with a PR emphasis. I currently live in Utah with my wife, Jennifer, and our 3 boys.

Connect with Mark Richardson
Here is my social media info:
Follow me on Twitter: depechefloyd
Smashwords interview:
https://www.smashwords.com/interview/depechefloyd28
Favorite my Smashwords author page:
https://www.smashwords.com/profile/view/depechefloyd28
Wattpad: depechefloyd

I really appreciate you reading my book! If you enjoyed this book, please encourage your friends to download their own copy from their favorite authorized retailer. Thank you for your support.

Printed in Great Britain
by Amazon